CAN'T GET ENOUGH

EROTICA FOR WOMEN

EDITED BY
TENILLE BROWN

FOREWORD BY
COLE RILEY

CLEiS
PRESS

Published in the United States by Cleis Press Inc., 2246 Sixth Street, Berkeley, California 94710.

Printed in the United States.
Cover design: Scott Idleman/Blink
Cover photograph: John Davis/Getty Images
Text design: Frank Wiedemann
First Edition.
10 9 8 7 6 5 4 3 2 1

Trade paper ISBN: 978-1-62778-034-6
E-book ISBN: 978-1-62778-051-3

CAN'T GET
ENOUGH

Contents

FOREWORD

Erotica is a tricky business. It usually concerns such subjects as love, lust or various shades of carnal desire. Tenille Brown, a veteran practitioner of the flesh print wars, has edited a sublime example of erotica, *Can't Get Enough,* dedicated to the worthy theme of "hot, steamy, mouth-watering sex," which will bewitch readers like a magical spell.

Desire, as interpreted by Tenille Brown, is a good thing. She issues a stern warning to her detractors that these stories are not enticements to "endless orgies and empty encounters," but a positive tribute to moments of pleasurable, smoldering sex that anyone can embrace in all its glory. Those reading these tales should not be afraid of catching the virus of sexual promiscuity.

Nothing in these stories smacks of psychosis with its patho-logical, compulsive behavior, manic episodes, substance abuse or dependence. The characters contained within them are having a great time without guilt or shame. Good sex in these pages doesn't take into account whether the man can be seduced or the woman is lovable. It's anything goes. Throw all the rules out. When willing partners are involved, anything can happen and fireworks can occur whether in public or between the sheets.

Although the editor states these stories were selected for the woman reader, there is something in them for men as well. A sense of free-spirited disregard for the traditional and the customary is dumped out of the window as the writers go for the max in trashing old stereotypes and clichés. Male readers should make room for this dose of powerful female hunger in their sexual vocabulary. It would do them well to absorb some of these prescriptions for satisfying their partners. Open themselves beyond limits and restrictions. Going beyond the notion of good pussy and a big dick can only expand their reach for great, sizzling, addictive sex.

An older woman I once dated said, "Good sex is like a drug. Once you have had it, it can make you do anything to capture that first high. If you're lucky, you can push past that point to something even better, even hotter, even crazier. When you get to that level, watch out! I've seen men and women jeopardize their jobs, careers and community standing just to get that good sex. Believe me, that feeling...oh man!"

In each of the stories of *Can't Get Enough*, the key ingredients are openness, boldness, self-respect and an erotic connection not often seen in the real world. These lovers are not afraid to become vulnerable or to accommodate each other to reach the highest pleasure available. None of these folks need prompting or permission to get off and to keep coming back for more.

For example, take the threesome that roars into a torrid sexual flame in Rachel Kramer Bussel's "Under His Watch," where ecstasy is all that matters: "Everyone had a role—Colin's to push his cock deeper down my throat, Josh's to tighten his grip on my hair and bring his legs to either side of me, and Leonard's to touch himself while he looked on. Me? My role was to simply be the center of attention, to take what each man was offering me."

Or the uninhibited woman, not a tramp, slut or any restrictive tag, in Jacqueline Applebee's "Rocket Fuel" who declares she loves dick and facials. "It's simple really: I can't get enough of cock. I love blow jobs, hand jobs, taking it up my arse or my cunt. I love the feel, the look and the smell of cock."

And finally, Lucy Felthouse's "When He Gets Home" gives the perfect blueprint for a complete, drenching fulfillment: "Touching his wife's nub caused her eyes to roll back in her head and her pussy to contract around his cock, which in turn caused his cock to throb and twitch inside her. He'd have to up his game if he wanted to make sure she came before—or at the same time as—him. Grasping the slippery and sensitive bundle of nerve endings between his finger and thumb, he rolled and pinched at it. Amazingly, it swelled further at his ministrations, and he looked up to see Nina stifling her own moans by biting down on her fist."

We are a country who loves to be in love, loves to be desired. However, we are puritans who want to be free of emotional and sexual restraints. The stories in this book hold some of the cures for what ails us, and contain some of the answers for our popular moral cages.

Tenille Brown and Cleis Press are taking a firm stand for an end to sexual repression at a time when opposition has been shrill and resistant to progressive trends going full tilt. Both parties are to be commended for such bravery in an atmosphere of madcap cookie-cutter conformity and Tea Party conservative dogma.

Enjoy *Can't Get Enough* for all its treasured worth. We all

INTRODUCTION: TOO MUCH IS NEVER ENOUGH

I'm not greedy. I've always been satisfied with my fair share, never asking for more than is necessary...except when it comes to good sex.

You see, I believe that the best sex is the sex that makes me want it again and again, and when I began seeking out stories for this book, I wanted them to evoke that same reaction from readers. I wanted erotica that would leave me not only satisfied, but wanting more. I wanted hot, steamy, mouth-watering sex. I wanted stories that took the theme and turned it on its head, and boy, did I ever get what I was looking for.

As my word count began bursting at the seams, I found myself anxious and wishing for the space to include more, but I soon realized that what had landed in my lap was precisely what it was supposed to be—a book jam-packed with stories that left me winded, wanting and hungry for more once I turned the last page, and that was what I wanted to present to my readers.

I was aware that the title of this collection could be misinterpreted, could hint at a theme of endless orgies and empty encounters, but that was what I wanted to avoid. I made sure the stories presented were not only hot and racy, but also sex positive.

I didn't even want to think about the phrase "slut shaming." On the contrary, this book is filled with characters who want it, love it and aren't ashamed to show it.

Take for instance Jack in Louise Blaydon's "The End of Sensible," who is turned on by the sight of his lover, Tom, in women's lingerie:

At the top of the stairs, Tom disappeared into the bathroom without a word, and Jack went quiescently into his bedroom to wait. Probably it was stupid, this—waiting for Tom to come out of the bathroom in his (god) girl's clothes, just so that Jack could (oh god) take them off him again, but that was the point, wasn't it? Maybe Tom shouldn't be the prettiest girl Jack had ever seen, but there it was.

Or Miel Rose's female lead in "Big Appetites," who experiences a moment of passion like no other when the fleeting thought of making a baby with her lover enters the picture:

She's looking straight ahead, drumming on the steering wheel, nonchalant. "It really gets me when you're all laid out for me, naked, your legs spread wide, and you pull me down on top of you and I slip my cock right up into your pussy. I can look right into your eyes as I rock my dick in and out of you, just the way you like it. That look in your eyes is so sweet, so fuckin' precious. It's like we're making love, like we're making babies, or some shit."

There is no shortage of lustful women here, but the men have a hot presence, too, as in Tilly Hunter's rough and dirty tale of "Mud and Pain" and Kissa Starling's devilishly ironic story about "Blue Balls."

There are insatiable couples in long-term relationships, as

in Rachel Kramer Bussel's "Under His Watch," Blair Erotica's "Embraceable You," and the playful couple in Allison Wonderland's "Strip to My Lou," and there are fly-by-night moments of passion such as Beatrix Ellroy's "Before They Burn" and Monica Corwin's "Sleepless Need."

I could go on, but I'd run the risk of saying too much, when simply turning the pages of this lust-filled collection will be enough, at least for now.

Tenille Brown
Atlanta, Georgia

BIG APPETITES

Miel Rose

Row is big, the biggest guy I've ever fucked. She towers above the majority of people, surpassing them in height as well as width. She takes up a lot of space; she can't help it. This has been true for most of her life, and you can tell by the way she holds her body, the confidence she exudes, that somewhere along the way she became used to it.

Her biceps are solid and beefy. I can barely wrap my two hands around them. When we are lying in bed I like to bury my face in her armpit and kiss out along the sensitive underside of her arm, trace her tattoos with my tongue. Her back is a paradox, a broad sheet of rock-hard muscles covered with soft padding. I've tried to give her back rubs with my tiny hands but find the territory too daunting, my elbows and knees way more suited for the work.

There is something specific and physiological that happens to me when we are in close proximity. She walks by and my heart beats hard at my blood, driving it to the surface. I swear I can feel every particle of air displaced by her motion sliding over my skin, it's so sensitive. She wraps her massive arms around me and I go limp, swooning like some wacked-out lady on the cover of a paperback romance novel. And when she rolls on top of me with my legs spread wide to accommodate her, it grounds me like nothing else. Being a big girl myself, she makes me feel small in a way no one has.

See, when I met Row I wasn't used to fucking people bigger than I was. For me, this took our power dynamic out of the theoretical. It took it from a place I went to in my head, giving myself up to someone's psychological domination, and turned it to a real live thing rolling around in the bed with us. In the heat of the fuck, with her holding me down, I can struggle all I want; the only way up is to ask. That's okay, though. Mostly I don't want up.

Row has big appetites. She eats more meat than anyone I've ever been with, devouring whole animals in one meal, it seems. I can tell it's good for her; it's what her body needs. Even with me being a vegetarian, it somehow makes me wet watching her rip apart a steak. She eats her meat rare, still bloody. She likes to ignore me while she's eating and I just sit there watching her, crossing and uncrossing my legs, squeezing my thighs together. She'll look over at me every now and then, licking the juice from her fingers, and say, "You hungry or what, baby?" Like it's the meat I want, when she knows damn well it's her I want to sink my teeth into.

It's not like she ever keeps me waiting long. Like I said, the guy has big appetites. She likes to fuck, all the time, day or night, public or private. That's okay, though. I like to fuck too.

Really, you can't take us anywhere. Try as our friends might, it just doesn't work out. Take us out for dinner or drinks, ten minutes into it she has her hand up my skirt and I'll wind up in the bathroom bent over the sink getting my ass fucked. Or, if I'm lucky, she'll be up against the wall with her pants shoved down, her fist in my hair, maneuvering my tongue all over her hard clit. We can't help it. We're both sluts, and together we're always horny.

Trying to drive anywhere is the worst. One time we even drove her truck into a ditch. We were going to her mom's house for dinner, a thirty-minute drive, but fifteen minutes into it she had me frantic. I had my panties off and everything.

It went something like this: .

We're going to her mom's house, okay? So, I'm getting ready, trying to look presentable. I like her mom a lot, she's a great lady, not uptight or anything, I just want to look nice. I put on a high-waisted skirt, a little below the knee, black, paired with a silk button-up blouse, a deep wine color. I top it off with a black cashmere cardigan, soft as a kitten's belly, that I scored at Goodwill. I button the top three buttons, but it's pointless. No matter what I'm wearing, Row always makes me feel like a total slut.

She picks me up in her piece-of-shit truck, you know the kind, held together with duct tape and prayers, with mileage pushing three hundred thousand. I grew up with cars like that, the ones my dad or brothers were always working on, trying to get them to pass inspection, trying to get just a little more out of them before they got retired to the back lot for parts. Even though I don't work on them much myself, I've soaked up a lot of knowledge just being around them, and I have a few tricks of my own. Like, you'd be surprised how many miles you can go with a pair of panty hose replacing a shredded fan belt.

Anyway, she picks me up. First off, she pushes her glasses up her nose and gives me a long, slow look up and down. There's lechery in her eyes, in the crook of her mouth as she shifts into reverse and says, "Nice outfit." Like I said, she makes me feel like a slut.

Next she starts talking; she knows she can always get me this way. It doesn't even matter what she's saying, it's how she says it. She could be saying anything in that smooth, deep voice of hers and my pussy starts weeping.

This time though, it's not just any old thing coming out of her lecherous mouth. She's telling me how every time she sees me in lipstick she can't help but think about having to scrub it off her cock after our dates, how she'd love to see those lips wrapped around her cock right now. We're going to her mom's, she's not packing, but does it matter? She just wants to see me worked up. I could hold out on her, but I don't. She's getting to me and she knows it. I start crossing and uncrossing my legs, squeezing my thighs together.

She tells me how good it feels to come down my throat. "You give really good head, you know that?" she says. "And, fuck, you're such a slut for it. You LOVE sucking my cock. You'd go for that shit anytime, wouldn't you? You can't get enough." It's true; I'm a slut for her cock.

I'm sitting as far away from her as possible, looking out the window. I can't look at her or it will be all over. This doesn't faze her. She can see me shifting in my seat; she can tell she's got me wet.

"You know, if there's one thing I love more than my cock down your throat, it would have to be my cock buried in that tight, wet pussy of yours." She's looking straight ahead, drumming on the steering wheel, nonchalant. "It really gets me when you're all laid out for me, naked, your legs spread wide, and you pull me down on top of you and I slip my cock right up into your pussy. I can look right into your eyes as I rock my dick in and out of you, just the way you like it. That look in your eyes is so sweet, so fuckin' precious. It's like we're making love, like we're making babies, or some shit."

This is a new tactic, and it throws me. I break my rule and look at her. She looks at me, kind of awkwardly, and that's how I know she is serious. Not like she doesn't genuinely love to fuck my pussy, but this is something different.

We look at each other for a second and then she's back on track. "That's when you wrap your legs around me, when you beg me to start fucking you harder, really fuck your pussy. You're so wet I can hear my cock slamming in and out of you. That's my favorite sound, that and your voice telling me to fuck you harder."

I decide it's all over. Like I said, I'm a slut, and Row really brings it out in me. I lift my hips and pull my skirt up around my waist. I slip my lace panties down and off my left leg, letting them dangle from my right as I prop it on the dash. I know I'm going to leave a nice puddle on her seat to add to the years of grime already accumulated there. I slip my finger between my swollen lips. Jesus, how wet I get surprises even me sometimes. I'm not looking at Row. Despite that sweet moment, I'm still pissed that she decided to pull this on the way to her mom's.

But she's looking at me. I can see her out of the corner of my eye. She pushes up her glasses, takes quick peeks at what I'm doing to myself. She licks her lips, unconsciously, runs her hand across the short hairs covering the back of her skull.

My clit is hard and slippery; I can't get enough friction going, but I keep stroking. I want to make this look as good as possible. I arch my back, stick my tits out. I unbutton my blouse, showing off some cleavage. I throw my head back and start moaning while I stroke myself faster, making sticky noises I doubt she can hear over the muffler.

My eyes are closed, but I can feel her gaze like it's a tangible thing. Then I feel her fingers brushing my thigh. She has to stretch a little to reach me.

"Get over here," she says, her voice sounding strained.

"No," I say, continuing to rub my pussy, rocking myself into my fingers.

"I said get the fuck over here," she says, her need making her voice, making everything about her hard. "Little girl, get your ass over here right now, or I'm going to beat the skin off of it the next possible moment I get!"

There are two things about this that we both know. One is that she is the only one who can call me little girl. Two is that I love it when she beats my ass.

So it's not because of her threat that I unbuckle my seat belt and scoot my naked butt over to her. She takes one hand off the wheel and wraps a thick arm around me. I've got my left leg scrunched against her side and my right thrown over her lap and hanging between the seat and the door. I start sucking on her neck, whimpering in her ear as I hump my pussy against her thigh. Her hand kneads my ass and then slips down my crack and underneath.

Her fingers slip into me, and I gasp as she starts to fuck me in this crazy position. My hand slides around her gut, squeezing her flesh, then goes to her crotch, rubbing her through her jeans. She groans and pushes down on the gas pedal, jerking us forward. She is trying her best to look forward and drive straight. Suddenly she grabs my hand and puts it on the wheel. "You steer," she says, as she buries her face in my cleavage, taking a chunk of flesh between her teeth.

"You are fucking crazy!" I scream. Truth be told, I don't know how to drive so well. Steering is only one small part of driving, you might say, and doesn't seem like it would be so hard, but maybe you've never tried it with fingers up your pussy and a large piece of your tit between someone's teeth.

It all happens so fast. I swerve, she slams on the brakes and we're in a ditch. It's actually a lot better than it might have been. There's no one else on the road, no cops behind us, no tree for us to crash into. The ditch isn't deep and we haven't flipped over. We're both kind of shook up though. We just sit there for a minute, panting, not looking at each other. Then Row growls deep in her throat and pushes me back onto the seat. Her fingers find my pussy again and thrust home. She throws my leg over her shoulder and fucks me hard and fast, just the way I like it, looking into my eyes, like we're making babies or some shit.

CRAVING THE BEST MAN

JoAnne Kenrick

I'm wet just thinking about him, can't concentrate on anything other than trying to remember the sensation of his lips pressed against my sex and his sharp whiskers pricking my sensitive skin.

I lose my grip on a half-empty wine goblet. It slips to the floor and shatters, the sounds of breaking glass piercing through me. *Damn it.* Everyone looks up. My OCD mother in her pristine white skirt-suit rushes to clean up the red liquid soaking into the lush cream carpet, and party guests pile around me, trying to engage me in their conversation about the secrets to a good marriage. *Perfect! Now I'll never get away.*

Throwing my arms in the air, I give up. I despise how my cravings have taken over everything, leaving me constantly focused on my wants instead of my needs. *Want. Yes, I want him right now, even as my mother mops around my feet.*

This is stupid. I'd taken hours to tease my hair into soft, spiraling curls. Pinned it up with cute diamond pins. I wore a new dress and shoes. I looked nice. So why would I want to ditch my sister's engagement party for him? That would be such a waste of a pretty frock. And it would infuriate the bride-to-be, not to mention my mother. Then I remember the pretty peach lace corset squeezing in my waist and giving the girls a boost and I feel a grin spread. Shouldn't put that to waste, either. Wiggling my butt, I relish in the tight pull of the G-string between my cheeks. He could be yanking that cord, pulling my knickers down to take me from behind.

I give in, can't stand here any longer pretending I'm all sweet as pie when all I want to do is fuck the best man...again and again. I decide it's time for a fix and swiftly exit the parlor of my mother's Victorian semi to go look for him.

He is leaning against the brocade wallpaper decorating the hallway. He smiles at me from behind his long, dark bangs, twirling his bike keys over his decorated ring finger.

I swear, he looks all the more attractive wearing that ring.

Fixing tendrils of hair away from my face, I stand tall and slink toward him. I feel silly; never was one to get that accentuated sexy walk right. With my curves, I probably look more like a wobbling jelly than a sexy vixen. But my pussy leads the way; I am a slave to my cravings and don't care how I look. He winks, turning me into a quivering pool of mush with the sex drive of a spring bunny.

"Hi, not enjoying the party?" he says, his voice all velvet and smooth.

I want him to grab me and kiss me hard. I want him to drag me into my father's office behind him so he can fuck me. I want...

"No." My pulse races. What might he do to me?

"Wanna get out of here, Amelia?"

"Yes, badly." I step forward to pass him. He grabs my wrist

and shakes his head, a smile so wide, teeth so perfect—the benefits of being a dentist, I guess. I'm thinking I'd like to reach up and lick his pearly whites, and my cheeks heat. "But I can't."

His grip tightens, hurts a little. I can't decide if I like the pain. "My motor is outside, we could go anywhere you like."

"I should probably go back to the party." I wiggle and pull my arm, hoping to break free from his grasp. I don't try that hard, as I'm not too sure I want him to release me.

"I can't stop thinking about you," he croons, dark brown eyes glaring at me, skimming my body and stalling at my chest. "Been wondering what's under that dress all evening."

"My sister will notice we're missing." I'm a little worried, but mostly I'm silently begging for this hunk to throw me over his shoulder, to claim me.

He grabs my other wrist, spins me around and pins my arms above my head. I'm against the wall, and he's leaning into me. His hard flesh is pushing at my delicate region, telling me his intentions are not honorable.

"Your sister won't notice anything other than being the center of attention." He puts his lips on mine and forces my mouth open with his tongue. I struggle to breathe, to keep my senses. His kisses deepen, and unbidden need throbs between my legs. A soft moan escapes me. I feel his mouth curl to a smile, and I wonder what wickedness he is imagining.

"I want you, right now." He pushes harder into me, slides his rough hand under my skirt and up my thigh.

"No, really, I can't do this. Everyone is watching." For the life of me, I can't think. Don't want to think. My sex is throbbing, distracting me, driving me to the brink of insanity and dampening my knickers.

He manhandles me into the office. It's dark. I can't see a

thing except for a line of light beneath the door. Metallic clinks echo, and I assume it's him locking the door.

"No, seriously, we shouldn't do it in here," I say. I wait in the darkened room. He hasn't made a move in what feels like five minutes. Shivering, not from cold but from nerves, I anticipate his touch. Crave his touch.

He turns the desk lamp on, his face illuminated in a soft orange glow from the bulb.

"Better in here than out there with what I've got planned." He takes the neckline of my dress in his big hands and tugs until the material weakens and rips. My new dress, ruined. I want to cry, I should cry. Be angry or something, anything other than be a horny slut. An impossibility right now with his gorgeous browns glaring me over. "Take your shirt off," he demands.

"It's like that?"

"Uh-huh...now do as your master tells you and strip."

"Yes, Sir." I slip out of my dress, my skin prickling as the cold air skims me.

He looks me over. "I like how the corset stops short of your nipples." Thumbing something on my father's desk, he hums a happy tune. Paperclips? A wicked grin spreads over his face. Uh-oh. He's thought of some amazing way to get my rocks off. Not good; I usually scream when he gets creative with pain delivery.

He bends the flimsy metal and wraps two clips around each of my nipples. My nubs harden at his touch, and tingle and tighten. Then a sharp pinch shoots from my breasts down to my crotch. *Ouch.* He's clamped my nipples. He licks the tips of my nubs peeking through the metal, and he moans all gruff-like. *Grr.*

"Want me to bend over?" I ask, impatient to relieve the throbbing ache in my pussy and desperate to finish fucking before anyone realizes I'm missing.

"Oh, you know it's naughty to tell me what to do." He

glances around, searching for his next makeshift torture device. Something catches his eye; a glint of mischief flickers across his irises. "Lie on the desk," he whispers, unzipping his pants.

I don't want to do as I'm told just yet. I'd rather wait to see his cock jut out. I've missed that hard, long shaft, and want it buried deep inside me.

Already, a pearl of precum is glistening on the tip of his shaft. I want to lick it off, to tease his head with my tongue, make him as desperate for release as I am. I slink toward him, but he shakes his head. I ignore his warning. In one swift movement, I've got his end in my mouth and I'm licking up the salty goodness.

He groans and hardens inside me. "On the desk, now," he orders.

This time, I do as I'm told and lie on my back, heels of my shoes digging into the wood. Crap, I'm sure Dad will notice those dents in the morning.

He nudges my legs open and traces the insides of my thighs with one of my father's bendy rulers. Each time, he draws closer to my moist slit.

He lifts it slightly, then brings it down my swollen mound with a playful spank. I yelp. He repeats the motion, harder. I yelp again. He teases me with the ruler, moving it in circles between my sensitive lips. And he spanks my pussy again.

"You like being naughty, don't you?" he croons.

"No, Sir," I cry, so desperate for him to be inside me.

"You do, you're soaking wet. Just look at the mess you've left on your father's ruler." He licks the length of it. "Hmm, so sweet. You should taste yourself."

I shake my head. "I'd rather taste you, Sir."

Climbing onto the desk and between my legs, he then forces himself inside me. I relish in how my entrance stretches to accommodate him. He's no small boy; he makes me feel full. Now deep inside, he rotates his hips and pulls out. Before I can react, he's placed his cock at my mouth. "Taste us both, go on. And suck it hard, baby. I want you to beg my seed to come out. Do it."

I don't really want to taste myself, but I can't resist his hard-on. I want to please him, want to draw him to ecstasy. So I wrap my mouth around him again and slide down his length. He's wet, and my juices are smothered all over him. The mix of my sweetness and his saltiness actually tastes pleasant and I lick him from his head down to his balls, cleaning my own juices off him. Then I suck on him. Using my hands and mouth in unison, I work him hard toward spurting his cum. He tweaks at the clips over my nipples, the pain shooting straight to my pussy. I scream out with the pleasure/pain tingles gathering in my tummy. He tweaks them again and the pain explodes, permeating my whole being.

"Hm, you give quite the blow job, honey. Now get up and bend over, fast. I'm ready to come," he orders.

I scramble to my feet, only too happy to oblige, knowing his always vocal orgasm will bring forth my own.

He spanks me with the ruler, then rams deep into me with his cock, momentum and grunting growing harder, faster.

His groaning and moaning makes me close to orgasm, too.

And then he squirts his thick, plentiful seed into me, warming me.

"Tighten those clips," he demands. I do as I'm told and cause pain to once again shoot to my pussy and make me come over his length. My muscles contract and milk him for all he has to offer. I scream out, enjoying the postorgasmic nirvana and already thinking of the next time I can steal away a few moments to fuck him.

Someone bursts in.

It's my newly engaged sister and she's gawking. "Can't you leave him alone for a minute? Christ almighty, Amelia, anyone would think you guys are newlyweds!" Her fiancé pops his head around the door and cops an eyeful of me naked and bent over with cum dripping down my legs. He smirks.

My sister tsks, pushes him out and leaves us to it, shutting the door behind her. His voice is muffled, but we can still hear him. "I can only hope we're as happy after five years of marriage."

"Ha, he should be so lucky. Hm, I needed that…nothing like fucking my wife in her father's office to make me come like a…" My husband pulls up his pants and spanks me. "I fucking love you, Amelia."

"And I you."

UNDER HIS WATCH

Rachel Kramer Bussel

I'd say I'm lucky—if I believed in luck. What I believe in is making your own luck, seeking out not a soul mate who will fulfill your every whim, but someone who will make you not only a better person, but a more fully realized version of yourself. In short, someone who will make you *feel* lucky every time you look at him, hear his name, think about him, touch him, someone who will make you dizzy with desire and thanking God whether you believe in a deity or not that you found him and he found you.

That's what I have in my Leonard. Leonard is nothing like the dashing playboy types I'd been with before I met him. Leonard was fifty-one, a self-made millionaire content to let the younger men and women he'd hired run his software company while he worked on his house, played elaborate games online, studied art and traveled on occasion. I was a stay-up-all-night, thirty-four-year-old bartender, more concerned with where I was going to party that night than my investment portfolio or settling down.

We were opposites on paper, but the minute we met, I felt something in me shift, from my head to my toes, down deep in my soul, my marrow, and I knew we were destined to be together.

I didn't care about the age difference, or the fact that, at six feet tall, I tower over him by four inches, without heels. I cared that when he looked at me in that way he did when he approached me shyly at a friend's cocktail party, I felt his gaze heat up my entire body. He was sweet and polite, no games, no lines, just appreciative as he poured me a flute of champagne. I felt that heat even as I knocked back my drink, leaned down and whispered in his ear that if he was up for it, I knew a cozy little closet were I'd fuck his brains out. He wasn't drinking, but he sputtered in shock, not used to women like me. For the record, he didn't take me up on it just then—by now, we've fucked in plenty of closets, but that night he simply let me do my thing, mingle and flirt and flit around the crowd, until it was time for him to help me with my coat, share a cab and a sensuous, deep kiss in the backseat and get my phone number.

What I said before is a lie, actually—I didn't know for sure that he was the man I'd wind up marrying immediately, not even when, three weeks later (his choice), he finally bent me over in his bedroom so my long brown hair brushed the floor, arranging us so our bodies aligned as his cock speared me over and over. He was worth waiting for. I still didn't know it when he touched my clit and made me see stars behind my closed eyes, but I was getting the picture. I was still aglow, barely able to make small talk. I recovered as I sipped coffee naked in his bed and we stayed up all night talking. When I climbed on top of him as the sun rose, I knew for sure this wasn't just a one-night stand.

And it hasn't been. We got married two months later, me in a red-lace dress with red-and-gold fishnets, towering above

Leonard in red-and-black heels, him in a traditional tux. On our Honolulu honeymoon, he got his first taste of what our married life would be like—men and women flirting shamelessly with me, whether he was by my side or not. It had happened before, but something about us knowing we wanted to be together forever made me feel safer in flirting right back, especially the more I realized that Leonard, rather than feeling jealous, got off on it in a big way. Leonard doesn't wear his kinks on his sleeve—in fact, I'd never have known just how naughty he was if we hadn't connected at that party—but he is as passionately perverted as I am in his own way.

We're a pair—though sometimes, we're more than a pair. The dirty little secret to how we make our three-year marriage work is that when I'm in the mood, I go on the prowl, while he keeps a watchful eye. One night in bed on our honeymoon, he whispered in my ear, "I saw that model and his girlfriend hanging on your every word; it made me hard to think about him bending you over a bed and taking you from behind with your head buried between her legs. Or just him and you…"

I pulled back to stare intently at my new husband. "Are you saying you wanted the cute little redhead?"

"No, honey, I'm saying I want you. But I also know that lots of other people do, and if you're into it, I don't want to deprive you. And, well, I'd like to watch you let out your inhibitions, go totally wild, with whoever you like, as long as I get to watch."

We implemented that rule on our honeymoon, and have been playing with others ever since. It's not an everyday thing, or even an every month thing; it's a whenever someone strikes my fancy thing. I'm a bit flamboyant, and he likes to blend into the crowd, which works perfectly. I never look like I have my husband spying on my flirtations; I can ease whoever I'm chatting up into the idea of joining me in bed, and once they're following every seductive smile I beam their way, I drop the bomb. Most men don't care who's watching as long as I'm giving them my full attention; some even get off on it as much as I do. I don't know if I'd feel as comfortable seeking out strangers to sleep with if it weren't under the guidance of my doting husband. Not only does he make me feel safe, he encourages me to be my most outrageous, wild self. We play off each other, the way a couple should.

Our hottest time happened recently. I was wearing a jade-green silk dress that dipped down just to the point where my pushed-together breasts met, revealing the kind of cleavage that could stop traffic. I'd piled my hair together with umpteen bobby pins, leaving my bare neck, shoulders and chest exposed. Leonard loves when I show off "the goods," as he calls them. "I want everyone to appreciate you as much as I do, baby," he told me early on.

We were at a holiday party for a company Leonard has invested in, one of those events that in reality is just another excuse to do business over cocktails. The only cocks I wanted to talk about were attached to two men I'd set my sights on when we walked in the door; I'd noticed them huddled close, the one with the scruffy beard with his lips next to the blond Adonis's ear. I stared until one of them looked back, at which point I winked and kept on going.

We'd arranged for Leonard to arrive before me. I glided toward him, hoping the two men were staring. "Hi, honey," I greeted Leonard, kissing his cheek. "I think I found out what I want for Christmas. They're standing in the back, by the door."

He pulled me close. I didn't need to see his crotch to know he was as interested as I was. We'd both been so busy it had been a while since I'd been with anyone other than him. I've found that while business requires careful calculations, when it comes to sex, the more spontaneous you can be, the better.

"Why don't you take your gorgeous body on over there and introduce yourself?" I did, right after I'd picked up enough cheese and crackers for three.

"Hungry, gentlemen?" I greeted them with a smile.

"I didn't know this party featured servers," said the scruffy one.

"Oh, it doesn't. I'm just here to serve the two of you. Cheddar?" I asked, holding up a cube. He opened his mouth, and I pressed the orange nibble inside. "And you?" I held a square of Muenster toward the blond. I fed it to him, then let my dress brush against the scruffy man's leg. "I'm Andrea," I said, not wanting to have to remember a fake name.

"I'm Josh," said the scruffy one, "and this is Colin. We're clients of the firm." I didn't bother giving my mini-biography; I wasn't feeding them cheese to get to know their minds better.

"Well, Colin and Josh, I wouldn't want to take you away from such a glamorous night, but I thought you might enjoy some private refreshments, ones that are, shall we say, too refined for such a large group," I said, before popping a bite of Swiss into my mouth.

"What's the catch?" Colin asked, as if there were no sane reason a woman would invite two incredibly hot guys to join her in bed. Maybe not in his world, but in mine, it was at least a possibility, though one I had yet to indulge in with Leonard (before him was another story).

"Well, there's a small catch, actually...I'm looking to celebrate the season with my own version of the three wise men. You see that shorter man holding a scotch over there? That's my husband. We have a deal whereby he lets me fuck whoever I want, as long as he gets to watch. And tonight I'm in the mood for...a brunette and a blond." I raised my eyebrows, then snagged Colin's glass, unsure exactly what was in it, but needing the liquid courage, I knocked it back. "I'll be over there. Oh, and my husband's name is Leonard."

I handed Colin his glass back, then walked away. It wasn't the most subtle come-on I'd ever issued, but who needs to be subtle when you're offering yourself up as a party favor? I'm not offended if my advances are turned down, because I know I have Leonard by my side. He's more than enough man for me, and we both know that. I hoped the men would join us, but I knew we could have plenty of hot sexy fun without them.

No sooner had I requested another champagne, than I felt a tap on my shoulder. It was Colin. "We'd like to...you know," he said, smiling politely at me, and then even more politely at Leonard. I wanted to grin back, but knew if we were truly going to have the kind of fun I desired, I had to set the right tone, one that made sure we were equally invested in having fun with one another. I wanted Colin to know that even if I was on my knees, mouth open, begging for it, I was in charge. I may be the kind of girl who can't get enough, but I do so with dignity.

I winked at Leonard, then turned to Colin and cocked my head, toying with the start of a smile. "Actually, I'm not sure I know what you and...your friend," I said, indicating Josh just behind him, "are saying. Why don't you tell me a little more clearly? You can whisper it in my ear." I moved close enough to his lips that I could feel his breath.

Just because I was acting bold didn't mean I ignored the shudder of excitement that swept through me when Colin took my order and ran with it. "We want to fuck you, Andrea, both me and Josh, one at a time, or both at once, while Leonard watches you. And I personally want to feel those beautiful lips of yours wrapped around my cock."

I struggled to stay composed when what I suddenly longed to do was sink to my knees. Leonard must have felt me trembling, because he grabbed my arm. I looked up at Colin, seeing him in a new light, his face now glowing with the energy he'd passed on to me with his words. "Meet us in nine-two-seven," I told him, "in five minutes. And make sure your cock is nice and hard. You too," I tossed toward Josh.

I pulled Leonard toward the door before I could lose my cool; that I saved for behind closed doors. We rushed to the elevator and were blessed with being its only occupants. "God, you're so fucking hot," Leonard mumbled before grabbing me for a kiss. This is what I most love about him—his ability to find me beautiful even when I'm about to do something so depraved. Some men fantasize about their wife or girlfriend with another woman, but often even the most sensitive guy has a jealous streak somewhere in him. Not my guy. With Leonard, the jealousy gene was reversed; he *wanted* to see me get down and dirty. When he broke the kiss just before the elevator doors opened, he said, "I bet you can take both of their cocks in your mouth at once. I want to see you try."

I was dripping wet as we entered the room and I whipped off my dress, which, while gorgeous and glamorous, wasn't appropriate for a threesome. I let my hair down quickly, tossing my head so it spilled down my back, and slipped into the silky white nightie I'd packed just in case I got lucky (Leonard indulges my lingerie lust but prefers me *au naturel*). I was touching up my red lipstick when Leonard cupped my ass, then warned, "You better put down that lipstick because I'm about to spank you. I think a nice red ass is a fine welcome gift for your new friends, don't you?" It wasn't really a question, because Leonard knows I love getting spanked anytime, anywhere. I dropped the shiny silver tube and bent over the table, his slaps heating my lower half. "Ow," I sobbed, loving the pain, and the knowledge that he was hitting me extra hard to show off how much I could take. Soon he was interrupted by a knock at the door. Leonard retreated to a plush chair in the corner, one perfectly placed for what was about to happen.

I pressed my bright-red lips together one last time in the mirror, then answered the door. Colin and Josh looked even cuter than they had earlier. "Welcome," I greeted them. "You can put your coats—"

That's as far as I got before Colin pulled me toward him and kissed me. "You better not have been teasing us in there, Andrea," he said, the roughness of his lips and tone setting me off. He shrugged out of his coat and pushed me to my knees, while Josh grabbed my hair and bunched it in his hand. I heard Leonard get up and move closer, but deliberately kept my eyes shut to better focus on the feel of Colin's dick, which he'd taken out of his pants and was holding, offering me just the tip.

Knowing my man was close by made my throat open, my muscles relax. It wasn't just that I wanted Leonard to be happy, though I did want that. There was something about him seeing me like that, knowing exactly how it felt to have my mouth in that position, that made it feel more like a foursome than a threesome. Everyone had a role—Colin's to push his cock deeper down my throat, Josh's to tighten his grip on my hair and bring his legs to either side of me, and Leonard's to touch himself while he looked on. Me? My role was to simply be the center of attention, to take what each man was offering me. What Colin was offering was quite impressive. His cock was thick and hot; as aroused as I was, it still made me drool.

"Andrea likes having two dicks in her mouth at the same time," Leonard blurted. It was half true; I'd gotten off on the idea countless times. Leonard and I had both spun wicked fantasies about my oral skills, my ability to swallow two men's come, but I'd never actually done it. I didn't know if I could, in fact, pull it off, but oh how I wanted to.

Josh bent down, nipping at my neck before asking, "Is that true? Is Colin not enough for you?" He massaged my ass as he spoke, and the warmth from my earlier spanking rushed back to my skin.

"I want you too," I managed to say, as I pulled away from Colin momentarily. Josh stepped back and pressed his leg between mine, before Colin pulled me toward the bed, every movement the most delicious kind of frustration. They placed me on my knees at the bed's edge, then stripped, stood and positioned their cocks right next to each other. Leonard perched on the edge of the bed, cock in hand, smiling at me when I glanced at him. There was a beautiful symmetry before me, dick on dick, but I didn't have time to fully appreciate it. They were both dripping and I leaned forward to lick Josh's slit, then Colin's. Soon I was going back and forth, before someone put his hand on my neck and coaxed both heads between my lips. I could only keep them there for a few seconds, but what glorious seconds they were.

We filled the room with our fierce panting. Colin came first, covering my face with his cream, which caused Josh to almost immediately do the same. "Bring her over here," Leonard commanded as the pair smeared their cream all over my face, then gave me their fingers to lick. I knew exactly what Leonard wanted and started sucking him just before he let loose in my mouth. I swallowed, then rose and led my new playmates into the shower, where we got clean, and then dirty, and then clean again.

Maybe I am lucky after all.

STRIP TO
MY LOU

Allison Wonderland

It's Saturday morning and my stomach feels sticky. On top of that, my legs feel listless, and on top of that is my husband Lou. Not only did he start without me; he finished without me, too. It isn't like Lou to be so thoughtless.

"The early bird gets the sperm," I grumble, rousing from slumber.

Lou laughs. "Thank you for the lewd awakening, but that sticky stuff isn't mine." Lou reaches for the plate beside my hip and punctures a flapjack with his fork. Gently, he glides the griddle cake across my middle, dabbing it in the syrup. It's a little like the gel I squirt on bumpy bellies when I'm performing an ultrasound, except it's warmer and...hotter.

Lou nibbles on the fluffy batter, smacks his lips, licks the maple off my midriff. When Lou makes me breakfast in bed, well, Lou makes me breakfast in bed.

"You're quite the dish, Blaire," he remarks.

"You're quite the sap, Lou," I return.

He sticks a kiss on my belly button. "Thank you, beautiful."

"Oh, what a beautiful morning," I mutter, rolling my eyes. My husband calls me beautiful all the time, as if it's my name. I pout about it, pretend it's just a pointless, predictable platitude and when is he going to tell me something I don't know already? But the truth is, when Lou gets mushy, I get gooey, and by this point my insides feel remarkably similar to that syrup he's slurping. I shake my head, flipping my frown like a pancake.

"That's the spirit," Lou applauds, clapping my thigh. "Grin and Blaire it."

"I suppose that's easier than having to grin and, uh, bare it."

Lou smirks, shudders, shrugs. "Not really. Stripping is no different than undressing." He nestles his chin against my navel. "There's nothing to it."

I stroke his shoulder. "I'd be nervous, too," I commiserate. "Hell, I'd be petrified."

"I am neither nervous nor petrified," Lou insists, but his voice resists, sounding high but not mighty.

"You could've fooled me."

"I did."

"No, dear, you didn't."

"You're right." I knew he'd relent. "It scares the pants off me." I knew he'd lament.

"That's the spirit," I cheer, fisting the air. "Undress for success."

Now before anyone starts thinking nasty thoughts, I need to point out that my husband is not a striptease artist, amateur or otherwise. He's a triple threat: actor, singer, dancer. A true talent, only don't tell him I said so because the man will turn redder than a spanked fanny. I don't know why my music man doesn't like to toot his own horn, although it might have something to do with the fact that he has me to toot it for him. (So much for not thinking nasty thoughts.)

Anyway, *The Full Monty* opens tonight. It's a musical about down-and-out steel-mill workers convinced they'll be in the money if they're in the nude. Lou is one of the star strippers.

"My diamond in the buff." I touch his cheek. "I'm so proud of you." I mean it, too, and he knows it, his face pink against my palm. (See, what did I tell you?) Lou's an awful lot like Bashful the dwarf, only taller. But when he's onstage, he comes to life like Pinocchio. And, hey, as long as Lou keeps his performance anxiety confined to the theater, I'll continue to support him a hundred percent.

"Um, tonight, at the show, I should mention... Well, just please keep in mind that audience participation is optional, not mandatory. If your hand gets anywhere near my...pelvic area while I'm performing, the hard part won't be taking my clothes off. The hard part will be not getting aroused."

"On the contrary—the hard part will be getting aroused."

Lou groans while I giggle. He takes a gulp of air, then a gulp of orange juice. "I loathe you," he tells me.

"I love you," I tell him.

"I love you, too."

"Three."

"Four."

"More."

Lou's lips touch my thigh. His lips are sticky, but then, so are mine. We complement each other so well. "I don't have to come," I murmur.

Lou snickers. He reaches for the bottle of syrup, holds it over me, squeezes until it squirts. The sap taps my belly, keeps flowing. "Sit up slowly," Lou instructs. "Don't scrunch your stomach or you'll ruin it."

I follow his instructions to the letter.

"I put an *L* on you," Lou croons to the tune of the Screamin' Jay Hawkins ditty, "because you're mine." He belts up. "Therefore," he continues, fixing me with a look that's both austere and sincere, "you have to come."

I laugh until my belly aches, then smile until my face hurts. "Okay," I say. "I'll be there with *L*'s on."

I got a big bang out of the show. With a little luck, I'll get a big bang out of Lou after the show. I deserve one—I kept my hands to myself, made sure I didn't accidentally arouse any of the hard parts in his pelvic area. However, some women in the audience, with their hornier-than-thou attitudes and suggestive suggestions, would have done well to follow my example. Because unlike them, I was on my best behavior. And now I want Lou in the worst way.

I try to maintain some semblance of self-control when he emerges from the dressing room, but it isn't easy. He's beaming at me and his dolphin-gray eyes are shining and they're just as radiant as his smile. Now he's got me in his clutches, flush against his frame so that I'm clinging to him almost as tightly as the light-blue T-shirt he's wearing. His chest fleshes out the shirt quite nicely, molding the material to his muscles. My heart bumps his ribs.

"I saw you leading the standing *O*," he murmurs into my hair.

"I'd like to see you leading me to a standing *O*," I counter, hugging harder. "In fact, any kind of *O* will do. This is no time to be picky about positions."

Lou loosens his grip. I don't have much of one on myself, either. "I take it you aren't bothered by my new sex-symbol status?" he asks, guiding me toward the door.

"Not at all." I slip my hand into his as he starts to walk

me home, just like he did when we were teenagers. "On the contrary—I'm hot and bothered by it. I don't have to follow that pesky look-but-don't-touch rule that everyone else does." To drive home my point, I pull my hand loose and goose him.

Lou looks gratified yet mortified.

"What?" I shrug. "Can I help it if I get handy when I'm randy? If you don't like it, then don't be so desirable."

The blush is back with a vengeance. "Thanks, beautiful," Lou says, always gracious when I'm salacious. My shy guy and I round the corner, approaching our favorite watering hole. "Would you care for a cocktail?" he offers.

"Are they a package deal?" I'd like to know.

Lou regards me as if I'm one garment short of a full monty. "The cock and the tail—are they a package deal?" I clarify. "Because the way I see it, they're kind of like Danny and Sandy in *Grease*: they go together."

"Good grief," Lou mutters, shaking his head at my persistent prurience. "You know, Blaire, I used to bring out the best in you. Now I just bring out the beast in you. I think I may be losing my touch."

"You can have mine," I propose, and press my palm against his abdomen.

Lou places his hand over mine, cups his so that our fingers are touching. "What in the world am I going to do with you?" he contemplates. "Besides the…well, you know, the obvious."

I tickle his belly. "How about an encore? Is that something you would do with me?"

Lou leads me up the walkway. "You mean a private show?" he ponders, easing the key inside the lock. "I'm afraid that isn't included in the ticket price."

"That's fine. Rest assured you'll get plenty of buck for your bang."

"You're a beast, beautiful," Lou says, and I can hear the affection—and the arousal—in his voice. He shuts the door behind us.

When one door closes, so does another. This time it's the door to our bedroom.

"Why do you do that?" I query, slipping off my flats.

"Do what?" he asks, and his innocence is genuine.

"Why do you shut the door? Ain't nobody here but us dickens."

Lou pushes his hands into his pockets, making his pants bulge in all the wrong places. "I just don't want opportunity to knock while we're...knocking boots, that's all."

"That's right," I play along. "Opportunity had better find a more opportune time to come and knock on *our* door."

Lou laughs. "It's just comforting, I guess. Reassuring. I like doing it, so that when we're...doing it, we're completely alone together. Stuck on each other, stuck in here. Stuck in a never-ending state of embarrassing statements. Blaire, shut me up, please."

I trap him in a lip-lock, effectively shutting his trap. Lou responds with a trap of his own: his arms. They fit around me snugly, securely, like a bodice.

"Blaire, darling," he addresses me upon release, "let me entertain you." Lou bows. It is gallant and grandiose and I can't help but feel like a princess.

Lou smiles, kicks off his shoes. "Wish me luck," he says.

I don't heed. "There's no need. You lucked out with me. You're going to get lucky with me. Better not push your luck."

"I'll take your advice," Lou agrees, "and give you a kiss." So saying, he places a preperformance peck on my cheek.

Lights up. Showtime. I lean back on the bed, supporting myself on my hands as Lou's hips begin to gyrate like Pelvis Presley. There is no music, just me and my private dancer, standing before me in his tight T-shirt and Herculean hubris. I can almost hear him humming, "Who's afraid of the Big Bad Wolf?" I used to bring out the best in him. Now I bring out the beast in him, too. I am definitely not losing my touch. Lou watches me watch him—or maybe it's the other way around.

He lifts his shirt, curtain rising until the stage is bare. His chest is impeccable: a landscape of crimps and grooves and sinewy delights. I admire the undulation of his muscles as he moves. He is awkward yet graceful, confident yet modest.

Liquid lust soaks my panties. Each tingle mingles with the next, until my body starts to vibrate and my hips begin to roll.

"Are you trying to upstage me, Blaire?" he teases.

"Lou, button your lip and unbutton your pants."

Lou buttons his lip and unbuttons his pants, and when they come off, he looks like the Michelangelo's *David* but with all the naughty bits covered.

"Now we know who wears the pants in this relationship," Lou remarks, looking pointedly at my black slacks.

"Yes, we do. And it isn't you." I take off my trousers. "And it certainly isn't me."

Lou approaches the bed and I sit up as his body enters my space, right where it belongs. I love him—with my eyes, my heart, my hands. I touch the decadent dents in his abs. I touch the sculpted silhouette of his legs, and the thighs that could squeeze the juice out of lemons. I touch the contours of his cock, that hefty bump tucked inside his briefs, which are bright yellow and terribly tacky.

"I hate it when you wear those. It looks like Pac-Man is eating your package."

"Everyone's a critic," Lou grumbles. "And that includes me, by the way. Blaire, my love, your underwear is an obscene shade of blue. You look like a tropical fish."

I glance down. "They are all wet, aren't they?"

Lou nods. He rids himself of his dreadful drawers and then rids me of mine.

I take a moment to marvel at my unclad lad. His cock is rather...spirited, with its stiff stem and rosy hue. "I can see why they cast you in the show."

"Because I've got spunk?" he speculates.

"Yes, although technically it's your Mary Tyler Moornament that's got spunk."

A slight spout emerges when I tap the shaft. Ah, wood that I could. And I can. So I shall.

We exchange positions and now he's seated on the bed and I'm seated on his lap. Our lips unite, stick together for a while.

Lou's cock knocks at the entrance.

"Come on in."

There's a snug tug and he's inside, feeling right at home. His hands scale my breasts and his lips caress my ear, sharing wishes and kisses and words like *Blaire* and *love* and *beautiful* and others that I can't decipher.

"I never understood why they call them sweet nothings," Lou ponders. "I think they should be called sweet somethings."

You got to love a man who wears his hard-on his sleeve.

Our hips move in harmony, my body thriving on the driving force of his cock. But it isn't frantic. Bodies bumping, blood pumping, hearts thumping, we make love, not haste.

His eyes meet mine, and I notice the way he blinks in time with his thrusts, which are restrained yet restless.

I grind my groin against his—mildly at first, wildly at last.

He bursts inside me, a hot shot of spunk that causes my body to twist and turn, like the funnel of a tornado.

I let Lou slip out, but not away. A part of him stays with me—it is thick and clingy and makes me think of maple syrup.

In its pursuit of sappiness, my hand wanders between my thighs, then to his midsection, where my digits loop and dip and draw Lou's initial.

Lou laughs, admiring my amorous artwork. "It's beautiful, beautiful."

"Thanks, Lou." My smile stretches all the way from my soul to his, where they mate, just like we did. "Coming from you, that's one *L* of a compliment."

ROCKET FUEL

Jacqueline Applebee

It's simple really: I can't get enough of cock. I love blow jobs, hand jobs, taking it up my arse or my cunt. I love the feel, the look and the smell of cock. But I absolutely, positively, adore everything about cum. Precum is a shiny, salty drop of promise. Spurts of cum feel like a champagne explosion. The rarest ejaculate of them all, postcum is like a precious essence that has to be treasured on the tip of my tongue.

People like to call me easy, like there's some merit in being difficult. I'm a friend, a lover and a good time all in one. I know what I want. I don't hurt anybody. When I get with a guy, everyone's a winner. And I do love getting with guys. My fuckbuddies included Steve, a cabdriver who worked erratic hours. There was Lester, a hospital orderly who liked to dress as his favourite comic-book characters at the weekend. And then there was Mukesh Singh, a librarian who hated his job, but refused to leave because it kept his parents from making him work in his uncle's restaurant.

I'd started to notice that my obsession with cock resulted in some strange side effects. I'd been seeing Mukesh more than my other buddies lately. Mukesh had long black hair and broad happy lips. His cock was a lovely length; not so long as to set off my gag reflex, but big enough to make me feel like I could suck him forever.

On one particular evening, I'd swallowed gush after gush of Mukesh's ejaculate. I couldn't keep it all in, but he kept on spouting forth the good stuff. We'd kissed after. That was when I felt a tingle deep inside me. My heart beat strong and fast. As I left his apartment, I saw my bus some way down the road. I started running, although I knew there was no way I'd catch it. The world whizzed by as my feet carried me at a dizzying speed. Much to my surprise, I ran straight past the bus. I had to double back to the bus stop so I could board it. I looked down at my feet and then back to Mukesh's home far in the distance. I was amazed.

I suppose everyone dreams of gaining superpowers at some stage of their lives. When I was a little girl, I'd watch colorful butterflies flitter around my garden. I used to wish I could join them in their dance. Well, I wasn't about to start flying anytime soon, but I was still exhilarated at the thought of what cum could do to me. I decided more experimentation was needed.

I turned up at Mukesh's workplace the next day. It was a small reference library with just enough rare books to make it a going concern. Mukesh was just about to go into the copy room when I caught him.

"Hey, Kim. I didn't expect to see you so soon." He patted his pockets, and then checked his mobile phone. "Did you send me a text?"

I pulled him discreetly into the windowless room, full of noisy copiers and printers. It was stifling hot in there. I fanned myself and undid a few buttons of my blouse.

"I need you, Mukesh."

My friend grinned and adjusted his tie. "Well, I am much in demand nowadays. All the ladies love me." He was so full of himself, but I tried to not get annoyed at the Mukesh Singh PR machine.

"Less talk. More cock."

"Now?" Mukesh looked around. "Here?" He looked like he was about to object for a moment, but then he puffed out his chest, and grinned even wider. "Damn, Kim. You sure are one kinky girl." Mukesh pushed the door to the copier room shut with his foot. His hand was at his belt a second later. I sank to my knees. Mukesh wasn't fully hard, but he was getting there. I kissed the head of his cock. It twitched against my lips. Mukesh tasted great. Even if his cum didn't have an effect on me, I'd do this every day if I could. I just couldn't get enough. I licked up and down, savouring the fragrant tang of his pale brown skin, all sea salt, cologne and precum. The copy machines continued to whir and clunk around us. The odd sheet of paper fluttered to the floor. Mukesh made low appreciative noises, but then he squeaked. His hand went to my head. "Shit. I almost forgot, my boss asked me to get a report ten minutes ago." His hand gripped my hair harder. I didn't know if he was trying to pull me away, or if he was holding on for dear life. "I've gotta get back to his office before he comes looking for me."

I ran my hand along the length of his cock, coaxing him to be quiet. I just had to taste his spunk. My wish was granted mere moments later when Mukesh erupted in my mouth. I swallowed once, twice. Mukesh staggered back against a large printer, groaning. I wiped the last traces of sticky fluid from the corner of my lips. I felt a surge of happiness flowing through me. I wondered if it was my new superpower, or just the fact that I'd blown my friend in a library.

Mukesh tucked himself back in. "Kim, you're gonna kill me."

"I hope not. I need you, mate."

Mukesh straightened his tie. "Look, I hate to come and go, but I have to deliver this report to my boss man or he'll have my head." Mukesh bent to retrieve a stack of papers from the printer behind him. "Shit. I think the last page of the report is stuck in there." He started pulling at a drawer on the large printer, but it wouldn't budge.

I had a sudden thought. "Let me try." I gently pulled at the drawer. The whole thing shot out into my hand and slammed against the far wall. My eyes went wide.

Mukesh looked at the printer, and back to me. "When did you get so strong?"

I looked down at my hands; they appeared ordinary enough. Maybe my friend's cum had done something to me after all. I took a chance. I gripped the side of the printer. I lifted the entire thing as if it weighed nothing at all. Mukesh scrambled backward to the door, his mouth open with shock. After a few astonished seconds he moved closer to me. "Do that again," he said with a smile.

Mukesh delivered the report to his boss, and then we both snuck out of the library. We went to Steve's home. I sucked my cabdriver buddy, and then lifted his refrigerator with one hand. After the initial shock and a string of expletives, he gave Mukesh a high-five.

I was a cum-powered superwoman! It was incredible. I had never needed a reason to enjoy cock before, but now I felt like I was on a mission, energized by primeval forces. Mukesh and Steve were over the moon too; I was rampant in getting them in the sack. They loved my transformation.

My third lover, Lester, took a different approach to the whole thing. I hadn't seen Lester in months. I was hungry for a taste of his good stuff. However he kept me at arm's length. "Kim, I've been doing some research on your..." He waved his hand in the vague direction of his groin. "I've done some research on your condition. You're not the first woman to be affected by the properties of spermatozoa." Lester loved to sound clinical. He clicked on his computer keyboard, bringing up an old-fashioned illustration that I recognized. "There's a guy I knew once who said Sleeping Beauty was awakened by ejaculate, and not a kiss."

I made a disgusted face. "You think Prince Charming blew his load over a sleeping woman?"

"Maybe the guy who told me that was a horny dog." Lester brought up another web page. "And then I found this." A photo of a very pretty woman appeared onscreen. "Meet Paula Carlton. Or the Amazon Punisher, as she sometimes likes to call herself." Another photo popped up. This time Paula was wearing a skimpy costume, but she had a fierce look on her face and a coiled whip in her hand. "I met Paula at a gaming convention. She was totally into me, I'm sure of it. Anyway, I was drunk as a skunk on a Saturday night, but she carried me back to my hotel room." Lester made a strange motion. "I mean, she just slung me over her shoulder and carried me to bed. I don't remember too much, but she told me she could do what you could. I didn't believe her until now." Lester sighed to himself, suddenly looking dreamy. "I thought she was just really strong. Boy, I wish I'd stayed awake long enough for her to ravage me." I hit him on the arm. "What I'm trying to say is, we should all meet and see if we can put certain theories to the test. If this is what happens to you when you're exposed to male ejaculate, what will happen when you get some from another woman?" He looked deadly serious. "Girls can squirt too, under the right circumstances. And that's why I'm keeping my dick out of your grasp." He gave me a rueful smile. "For science."

I looked at the photo of the Amazon, surprised at a new stirring inside me. I'd only been intimate with a woman once before. It was nice and all, but I'd never thought too much about it. Now I pondered the idea of being with Paula, and I found it excited me. I just had to meet her.

Lester organized it all. I sat in my apartment several weeks later, feeling incredibly nervous about meeting the new woman. I wasn't even sure what to call her. Addressing someone as Ms. Punisher seemed a little formal.

I wore strappy heels and a short flirty dress that was feminine in the extreme. My reddish hair was styled into a mound of soft curls. Dangly earrings and a dusting of makeup completed my outfit. I wanted to impress upon Paula just how womanly I was. I didn't want her to see me as any kind of a threat.

My three lovers lounged about on the floor, all tapping away on their cell phones and their tablet computers. They hardly paid me any mind. That all changed when Paula arrived.

The Amazon barreled into my room with a look of outright lust on her face. "Lester was right. You're gorgeous," she said breathlessly. "We've got to have sex immediately."

"What?" I squeaked. "Don't you want to talk about our abilities first?" I tried to step away, but Paula dragged me into an embrace. "We could all have some coffee and a chat. How's that sound?" Paula ignored me. She just nuzzled the side of my neck.

My three lovers all stood wide-eyed with shock.

Mukesh was the first to speak. "I think you should have sex too."

Steve was practically buzzing with excitement. "Yeah, it will be great to see what happens when you get some woman's cum inside you."

I looked to Lester. "This has got to be a dream," he whispered. He ran to his satchel in a corner, pulling some equipment out. "We have to film it too. For the sake of science."

I managed to break free from the Amazon. "Okay. I'll agree to the sex." I glared at Lester. "But not to the filming."

My mandate didn't seem to bother Lester at all. "Fine. I'll just take detailed notes." He was such a nerd.

I turned to Paula. "Are you certain about this? You don't know anything about me."

Paula pulled me close once more. She was gentle as she ran a hand over the bare skin of my collarbone. "I've felt like such a freak for ages. Everyone's too afraid to get close. I longed to meet someone like me." She kissed me briefly. "And now that I have, it's impossible to keep my hands off you." She smiled at me. "I just can't get enough." Paula seemed so earnest that I couldn't resist her. I felt myself relax in her arms.

I kissed Paula lightly on the lips. I felt her fingers travel down my back as I dotted little kisses all over her face and neck. We moved together slowly, dancing a slow-dance of desire that grew with every passing moment. We maneuvred our way to my sofa, landing in a heap. Paula squeezed my breast with a gentle touch. I was really glad that she had calmed down some. This would only be my second time with a woman. I didn't want to get it wrong. I wedged my knee against her cunt. I could feel the wiry curls of her pubic hair. Of course the Amazon wouldn't wear knickers. Paula made a low groan. She ground herself against me as I pushed a little harder.

"I think you should both aim to climax simultaneously," Lester called out. Mukesh and Steve hit him, urging him to be quiet.

I turned my attention back to Paula. She drew up the hem of my dress, pulling it over my head in a sweep. My hair became tangled, but I didn't care at all. My initial apprehension at being with a woman had vanished once she got me naked. I sat astride her hips and then bent down to kiss her again. Paula's tongue touched mine. I sucked on it just like I would suck on a cock. It was absolutely delicious. I could have continued that endeavor all day, but I suddenly jolted upright as Paula's fingers nudged my clit. She circled me with sticky fingers, and then she plunged inside with a welcome thrust. I surged atop her as she added another finger inside me. I reached up to squeeze my own tits, rolling a nipple between the fingers of each hand. I'd never expected any of this, but I was suddenly glad that my obsession with cock had brought me here.

"You are a goddess," Paula breathed. "Please let me suck your pussy."

All three men groaned out loud at that statement. I spared them a brief glance as I got comfy in a new position, flat on my back on the sofa. My lovers each had a hand in their trousers. Mukesh looked as if he were about to explode. Well, it wasn't about men's cum anymore. I was determined to make Paula give me some of her good stuff too. I turned her so we lay in a sixty-nine pose. I had about a second to see her furry cunt above me, before she lowered herself onto my face. I breathed in her warm scent, and then set to work licking and sucking her labia and clit. I used two fingers inside her, just as she had done to me. Paula's sticky fluids coated my face. It felt like I was being bathed in cum. It was wonderful.

I felt a fiery sensation build in my cunt as Paula brought me closer to my orgasm. I tried to concentrate on what I was doing to her, but in the end I just gave myself over to it. I shook beneath her as I was rocked by a massive climax. After a few blissful moments I sagged back on the sofa cushions. Paula eased herself off me, looking very satisfied. I was pretty pleased too.

For my second time with a woman, I hadn't done too badly.

Paula put two wet fingers into her mouth. I knew she was sucking on my cum. For some reason it made me pulse with an aftershock. I looked down at my own fingers, took a breath and then did the same thing.

I felt my pupils dilate as I sucked my fingers clean. My skin grew impossibly hot. I looked at Paula and knew that she was feeling the same way. My toes curled with the intense pleasure that rushed through me, even though I was sore from my orgasm.

Paula held my hand. I could feel tremors through her finger-tips, a fluttering lightness that mirrored my own response.

Lester shook his head. "I don't know if anything new happened, but that was amazing. Just think what it would be like if we had an orgy!"

Mukesh and Steve suddenly broke out of their shocked state to grin at me.

Lester scribbled in his notebook. "We could take it in turns to come inside you."

"You'd be unstoppable!" Mukesh said with enthusiasm.

"Let's make it happen." Steve started unbuckling his belt.

Paula nodded her head. She smiled a lovely smile at me, not looking remotely like an Amazon Punisher. I was just happy to have more sex with some good people. I'd always known I couldn't get enough cock, but now it appeared that I couldn't get enough cunt either.

I pulled Paula along with me as we rushed to my bedroom. And if our feet moved light and quick, it wasn't just our speed. It was because gravity had no hold on us. It was the best and only way to fly.

HIS SUBJECT

Madison Einhart

S tay still." His voice was so commanding, so matter-of-fact. Anything less would be unacceptable. Carter sat high on his stool, positioned in front of a stained, wooden easel. An over-sized canvas hid all but half his body—that white dress shirt with its share of paint stains, haphazardly rolled up against the thickness of his arms. His jeans were equally war torn, a spatter of orange here, yellow there. He sat with his knees cocked, feet resting on his oak throne. With a long drag from his cigarette, he lifted his loaded paintbrush to his painting once again.

Carter was a stern man. Being an "artist" came with a lot of unfortunate stigmas—a lack of money, a lack of work, a lack of respect—but the only black marks allowed in Carter's life were self made, purposely, in his compositions. He was an exhibition champion, a gallery feature, a master. His posture, his sneer, they all reflected his unwavering confidence. There was always such intensity in the depth of his dark, brown eyes. He stared at his canvas like an enemy, like an obstacle to overcome. Even his brushstrokes were visibly confident. They always were, just as his curly brown hair always looked a disheveled, frustrated mess. There wasn't time to brush the stray hair out of his face. He was far too busy taming the monster that was his creative intent, forcing the canvas to do his bidding. Leaning to the side and peering at his subject once again, he frowned.

"Rebecca." There was depth and richness to his voice. He was such a tall, broad-shouldered man, and the height of the stool only made him more ominous. His unforgiving eyes focused on her, scanning once again. Nothing was worse than an uncooperative model—except maybe when said model was also your wife. "Stay. Still."

But it was terribly difficult to stay still. Carter had positioned Rebecca on a worn sofa, sprawled out on her back...naked. Completely naked. No draped cloth, no turning her back to him. She was fully exposed, full figure and all. Her only hope was the long, black hair that spilled over her shoulders. A collection of raven curls dangled at her plump breasts, but they didn't come close to offering ample coverage. In fact, when she tried to employ some tasteful strategy, Carter only demanded a more provocative position. She was completely at his mercy, and the chill of the open studio teased her exposed, olive skin. In fact, it made her really wet. It always did. These lunchtime rendezvous only ended one way, and her body was well aware. Carter was outwardly rather cold, but how he loved to appreciate her body—how he loved to make her wait. Time and marriage had done nothing to dilute their lust for each other.

"I'm sorry," she said, her green eyes wandering away from his. The cheekiness in her voice always bought a smirk to his lips. She knew it. She didn't have to look. He knew she wasn't *really* sorry. "I'll try to stay still, Carter."

But Rebecca was short on time. Thirty more minutes meant

the end of her lunch break. Thirty more minutes and she would be expected to be in her office, at her desk. She, too, was an artist—it was how she and Carter met, so many years ago—but Rebecca had largely taken the commercial route. She was an art director at a prestigious design firm. Her life was filled with logo designs, business cards, and websites. Her dirty, painter's smock was replaced with pencil skirts, blazers and heels. Carter loved that about her—Rebecca was a hardworking woman with a ball-buster reputation. With her own office and her own team of designers, her portfolio was regularly an object of envy. This lifestyle often meant long hours, but it came with great financial success. However, this also meant canceled dates, and Carter was not one to be abandoned without consequence. She'd have to make it up to him, and she'd have to do it his way...every lunch break for the next month. There was no debating this contract. Despite their differences, one thing was quite clear: above all else, she was undeniably his. He wasn't about to let her forget it. Little had Rebecca realized how addictive this contract would become.

Of course, she resisted at first. She always did, but the excuses were in vain. In fact, nowadays, she did so on purpose. It was fuel for his hungry, fiery eyes. She'd strip off her business attire, piece by piece, every afternoon, and pose for her Michelangelo. It was a willing, wonderful contract that occupied her mind throughout the workday. Just wait until noon. Contain yourself until noon. It was *very* difficult to focus on anything else.

A frustrated grunt interrupted her inner dialog. She turned her head, purposely moving to look over at her husband. Carter was looming with crossed arms. As he stood beside his canvas, Rachel desperately tried to force her eyes away from the tight jeans hugging his hips. Just observing his body's girth stole her breath; how easily she could remember his strength against her smaller frame. His sun-kissed skin, his wrinkled shirt, his five o'clock shadow, his worn, dirty hands...

"You model like a novice." Carter approached and placed a hand under her chin. He guided her face back to its proper place, away from him and his canvas. "Either that or you enjoy my frustration."

Her body tensed, eyes on the ceiling as she tried to follow orders. Unexpectedly, she felt the soft fibers of a paintbrush against her skin, brushing, teasing, tracing her features. Carter paid great attention to her collarbone. Inching down her body with precision, he paused only for a moment between her breasts. The brush lifted, and she found herself lost in anticipation. Rebecca tried to turn her head to see him, but he only redirected her glance away once again. "Stay still."

The bristles fluttered against her breasts, one after the other. Every so often, he would slyly brush at her nipples, an accidental flick against the hardened mounds. Her back arched, easing toward him. There was no need to beg. Her body so visibly wanted him: those curled toes, the way she'd bite at her lips. Carter knew, and he savored it. Staying still was obviously difficult for her, but his slow strokes were visibly torturous. Carter was well aware that time was not on their side—well, at least it wasn't on *Rebecca's* side.

Her cell phone chimed. It was the twelve-thirty alarm. It was time to get back to work.

Rebecca turned, looking at Carter with urgency. There was no need to exchange words. Her eyes begged, but his eyes refused. She could feel the smooth, finished end of the paintbrush toying with her moist opening. She was staring back at him in silence; his breath was heavy, his brow was tense. The smooth, wooden surface of the handle slipped inside of her. Its finger-like width slid rhythmically back and forth. Rebecca's head tilted back and she allowed herself a long, satisfied groan. "Carter, please."

"Commercialism has made you an impatient woman." He was amused with her. "The best things in life are to be savored, Rebecca. The process is just as important as the finished product, and mastery takes time."

It was the same lines he'd give at a gallery opening. It was the same logic he'd profess to students. Rebecca leaned toward Carter, defying his commands, digging her fingers into his unruly curls. They shared a heated murmur as their faces drew close, but the situation was far beyond words. It was a hunger that had possessed them for years, satisfied only in each other's warmth. Friends and family had teased that their puppy love would be a passing intoxication. Little did they realize how passionately and absolutely in love Carter and Rebecca were; the intensity when their lips met, the hunger as they kissed each other, was as vibrant and colorful as on their first rendezvous. The paintbrush slowly left her inner warmth, dragging against her opening. She was more than ready, and judging by the visible firmness in his jeans, so was he.

Her damn cell phone began to ring. How much time had passed? Was that the office? Rebecca slowly unbuttoned her husband's shirt, and she savored the definition in his chest. Button by button, down to his pants; the phone's ringing was meaningless. Her eyes traced up him; he was staring down with overwhelming need. Moments like these could have served as payback, but unlike her lover, Rebecca could never quite contain herself for long. Maybe Carter was right. Maybe commercial art had made her an impatient woman. She unbuttoned his pants, shifting and toying with his clothes before wrapping her fingers around the width of his firm shaft. She stroked him, their eyes locked. Carter's face was overtaken with lust, as he grunted under his breath. Her fingers knew to tease his thighs. They knew the rhythm that took his breath away. The only means of heightening his ecstasy lay within the warmth of her mouth. Leaning forward, she kissed his cock, running her tongue up its length and flicking beneath the rim. Carter clenched his teeth, and his hands worked themselves into his wife's long raven curls. He pulled at her, moaning her name with such unapologetic passion.

Together, the two stood up, breathing in a moment of silence before Carter lifted his wife. The strength of his arms left her feeling weightless, pressing her back against the cold studio wall. Her legs wrapped around his waist. Arms around his shoulders, fingers clenched against his back, her large breasts squished into him. Skin on skin, his hands had a firm grip on her ass. Leading himself into her moist, eager slit was easy. Too easy, as she whimpered and tugged, desperately. It was his breaking point. At this stage, it was difficult to savor and much more enticing to devour. Carter's hips pushed upward and into her with an animalistic intensity. He lifted and lowered her with such ease. Her skin slapped against his with each rough thrust, and her lustful cries only drove him further.

The two of them were beyond dirty talk; their bodies were an extension of each other. When her moist walls tensed against his shaft, he knew it, he felt it, and he knew what it meant. Rebecca liked it *this* way. Making her climax was one of his greatest pleasures—that look in her eyes, the way he could make her sing. Nothing else sent his pulse into the same heated frenzy. Pulling her from the wall and laying her on the worn couch, he mercilessly ravaged her. Rebecca's voice filled the room—and Carter lost himself, filling *her* up, overtaken by his beautiful wife.

It was nearly four o'clock.

MUD
AND PAIN

Tilly Hunter

Dean was ahead already. I admired his ass as his soaked shorts clung to its contours. He was always faster than me, although in a race like this anything could happen. We'd trained for months for the ultimate endurance test, the Toughest Ten, bored with marathons and ironman triathlons. It was Dean who first turned me into a fitness freak. After spotting him lifting weights at the gym I found myself going more and more often in the hope of bumping into him and being able to watch him putting his magnificent body through its paces. It was the body of an underwear model. Or perhaps a sculpted Greek god.

One day, after we'd graduated to swapping names and terse hellos, he said to me, "Hey Joe, how about doing a marathon with me?"

"Sure," I said, before engaging my brain. The most I ran was half an hour on the treadmill, never outdoors. I was just blessed with a naturally toned physique that looked like it saw the inside of a gym far more than my actual couple of hours a week. He soon realized this. But he was patient, quietly sharing training tips, chivying me along when my spirits flagged and coaxing me to push myself, without ever sounding patronizing.

I guess it was the chemistry between us. He wouldn't have put up with me otherwise. Sometimes he slipped into sergeant-major style, even name-calling: "Come on you worthless faggot, get your butt moving before I order the lads to give you a beasting." It was all playacting. He'd been in the army for a while. He told me he left because he enjoyed the rough treatment too much. He feared for his well-being. And that was the funny thing about our relationship as it became intimate. He was stronger, faster and could endure far more than me. But it was me who got to wrestle him to the floor, grab handfuls of his hair, slap him and call him my bitch. He responded in an immediate physical way, going weak at the knees, eager to drop and suck my cock or let me pound into his ass mercilessly.

"Fuck, Joe," he'd say, "you do things to me. Things I haven't been able to experience with any other man."

He knew I'd be watching him as he pulled ahead in the Toughest Ten. It wasn't just a run. It was a ten-mile course with ten obstacle stages—mud, ice, fire, water, walls and more to crawl, swim, wade or climb through. Designed by the military's elite, it put those crazy enough to attempt it through hell and provided the best endorphin buzz available without mind-altering substances.

Our training had covered most of the types of challenges we faced. More thoroughly than necessary, to be honest. I'd confidently bet none of our competitors had submitted to having their balls zapped in order to prepare for the electric fence field, where you had to hurdle or otherwise climb over a dozen electrified wire barriers. Dean saw it as an opportunity to expand our collection of toys. He invested in a "humbler" device that locked his balls tight within a bar that curved around the base of his buttcheeks, keeping him bent over on all fours. It could be hooked up to an electro-stimulation unit with a nine-volt battery.

I tried it once. Once was enough. He loved it. Reveled in seeing how much he could endure. It made his cock hard and his ass gape. I made sure to turn off the power before I took him. It was always me who called time long before he'd give in.

But the electric challenge was last in the race. Right now I saw him plunging into the next one, a deep, wide pool of ice cubes. Like a kids' ball pool, only a lot less fun. He waded through, arms wide, broad shoulders battling. I tried not to think about how it was going to feel. We'd filled my bath with ice and lain in it until we were numb, but I knew moving in this was going to bring a fresh stab of torment with every step. I jumped, arms flailing. Shit. I felt the shock deep in my cerebral cortex.

I didn't want to move. I didn't want the ice to touch new areas of skin, to soak through new patches of Lycra and nylon. I focused on Dean's solid shoulders as he hauled himself out of the far end of the pool. He glanced at me, grinning insanely, before dashing off to the next obstacle, a crawl through mud under a low cargo net. I willed myself to lift a leg and lean into the ice, to paddle a way through with my arms. My body was losing sensation, my teeth starting to chatter. I'd gone from sweating with exertion and adrenaline to shivering uncontrollably. I fixed my gaze on a spot at the far end, a tiny dent in the wooden frame of the pool, and pushed toward it. If I stopped any longer, I'd probably never move again.

I reached that spot, touching a finger to the dented wood, and dragged myself over the side and out. Ice is meant to be good for tired muscles, but they just felt tight and heavy. I stumbled on, a mile to run before the mud. Dean was probably already through it.

Occasionally I passed another competitor, mostly male, and the odd lean and muscular woman. Or I'd run past someone doubled over at the edge of the field, clutching a stitch. But then I saw the next obstacle and all my attention was taken by Dean, stopped on his belly under the rough rope netting as if he was in trouble. He was certainly in danger of getting crawled over if the main body of runners caught up.

He was covered in mud, up to his elbows in it, the front of his clothes stained, thighs darkened, face splattered. And that rope, pressing into his shoulders and one coarse strand cutting across his face as he looked back toward me. He loved rope. Loved to be tied up tight while I used his body roughly. I thought I was already riding an adrenaline high, but a special injection of chemical energy shot straight to the base of my cock at the sight of him.

I ducked under the net and slithered and crawled along. It was pulled too low and too tight for me to stay on hands and knees and I found myself on my stomach, clawing my way through foot-deep filth. It stank of mold and sulfur.

"What's wrong?" I shouted, as I slid toward him.

He just stared at me over his shoulder with his mouth open and a dark look in his eyes. He was muddier than necessary, really. As if he'd deliberately writhed in it. I reached him and placed a hand on his arm. "What's up? Are you hurt?"

"No. Not hurt. But I feel incredibly fucking horny and I want your cock inside me."

"What, here? I can't fuck you here. And what about the race? Let's finish, then fuck."

"I can't wait. It's the mud, the rope, the stench, everything. I need you. I need you on top of me, in me."

His words made the blood rush into my shaft. My cock strained inside my tight shorts. "I'll fuck you," I said. Dean groaned. "But we do it in those bushes. If only to avoid being trampled. And then we finish the race."

"Yes," he said. "Let's go."

He commando-crawled the remaining length of the net. I followed closely, watching the flex and bunch of his muscles, the splatter of mud farther up his body, as I struggled, out of breath, to keep up. Dean ran through gorse and nettles to the stand of thick shrubs off to the side. I hoped no one was watching us. Maybe they'd think we were taking a piss stop. But together? I realized I didn't really care.

Thorns scratched at my shins and nettles prickled the reddened skin. I pushed through to where the bushes hid us from the track and Dean grabbed me and pressed his lips to mine. He held the back of my head tight in one hand and grabbed my butt with the other, pulling my crotch into his, hard cocks colliding through the constricting fabric. I pulled away with difficulty against the strength of his arm. "Shorts down and on your fucking knees," I ordered. "Now."

He pushed the shorts right off, showing a patch of white between the mud on his thighs and that on his belly, and dropped to the earth, facing me. His cock was fully hard. I pushed my shorts down to let him see mine spring out, pulsing bigger as it was freed. "Turn around and get your face to the ground," I said, not letting him taste my cock although I would have enjoyed it. I wanted to fuck him, but I also wanted to finish the race. And not in last place.

I knelt at his butt, feeling cold grass crushed under my knees, and let a string of saliva fall from my mouth to his crack. I rubbed it downward with the tip of my cock and he moaned, rocking his hips against me and pushing his ass muscles out hungrily. He had his hands braced on the ground and his forehead pressed to the damp earth. Knowing that he wanted me this badly made my throat tighten.

I mouthed my palm, moistening it and then transferring the wetness to my shaft. I pressed the tip of my cock against his dark hole, giving him only a second to relax before I pushed in farther. I slid my shaft in relentlessly until my pelvis hit his cheeks and I began to pound him. Dry skin dragged, my hurried attempt at lubrication not entirely effective.

"Fuck," he groaned. "I need this so badly. I need you. To fuck me hard."

"I know."

I gave him exactly what he needed, driving into him fast and deep. In a flash of inspiration, I grabbed his shorts from the ground, wrapped my hand in them and tore off a handful of nettles from beside us.

He sensed my rhythm changing and twisted his neck to see what I was doing. "Eyes down, slut," I said. He began to groan continuously. He probably wanted to take his own cock in his hand but would wait until I gave permission. If I gave permission. I pushed his T-shirt up his back, bunching it at the nape of his neck, and brushed the nettles across his shoulders. His ass clenched tight around me as he gave a strangled cry of pain. "Open your hole, slut," I said, moving the nettles to his ass and brushing them over his right hip and buttcheek, watching red bumps rise on his skin. He shuddered as he fought to keep himself open. I grasped his left hip and pumped him faster while I played the nettles over his back with my other hand. Just once I caught the stinging leaves on my thigh and yelped at the sudden stab of poisonous pain.

Hyped up as I was on the adrenaline of the race, my climax started to build quickly, balls tightening and cock thickening to split Dean's hole wider. I slowed a little. "You can wank your-self now," I said. "And make it quick because I'm going to come soon and if you don't catch up you'll have to wait until after the finish line."

He shifted his weight onto one forearm and took his cock in the other hand. I grasped him with both hands, the nettles dancing over the tender side of his belly and ribs, and pulled him back onto me as I fucked him with long, measured thrusts to give him time to get close. But I was desperate to fill him with my spunk. The thought of it dribbling from his ass as he crossed the finish line had me right on the edge.

"I'm going to come," I groaned. I felt him speed up his hand, guttural sounds coming from his throat with every fast breath. The come surged into my shaft and I pumped him with hard, juddering thrusts as it spurted along my length and out inside him. He came onto the earth with one long moan.

I slipped slowly out and rose, pulling up my shorts. Dean stayed on hands and knees panting. Waiting.

"Rub your face in it," I said. He shuffled back and bent his head to the pool of white on the soil. He pressed one cheek into it, then the other, and rose to show me. Come mingled obscenely with mud and sweat. "Now put your shorts on and let's go. We have time to make up."

I ran off, leaving him to catch up with me. He was soon beside me, easing to my pace as we ran to the next obstacle, narrow pipes we had to crawl through for an agonizing, muscle-cramping three hundred feet of dark claustrophobia. It was one we hadn't really been able to prepare for. We didn't know how far back in the field we now were, although a quick glance showed there were still some people limping along behind us.

We stayed together, Dean waiting for me to emerge from the pipes and then slowing his pace to match mine. My fitness had come a long way since our first marathon and we gradually edged up the field, eventually passing the main mass of competitors on the second to last obstacle. We launched ourselves at the electric fence hurdles without pausing to consider the pain to come. It was impossible to clear them without getting zapped— inner thighs, butt, balls.

We crossed the finish line and were handed medals and bottles of water. A screen flashed up our time and position. We'd come in 67 and 68 out of a total of 470. The winner was only twelve minutes faster. I realized we could have won, but I wouldn't have missed our detour for the world.

As we applauded at the awards ceremony, I grabbed the ribbon holding Dean's medal around his neck, twisting it tight and pulling him toward me. He gasped in that desperate and endearing way of his. All the competitors were filthy and sweaty, but come had dried to a flaky film on his cheeks alongside the dried mud. "I think you got off lightly in the electric fences because you're taller than me," I whispered. "When we get back to my place, I'm going to lock your balls in the humbler while I have a nice, hot shower. When I'm done, I'm going to hook you up to the battery and sit back with a beer until you beg for mercy."

"Let's go now," he said.

THOSE
DAMNED
COBBLES

Tamsin Flowers

Toward the end of the afternoon, you send me a text. I'm in the office and as I surreptitiously check my cell beneath the cover of my desk, your words set the heat rising within me.

Home already, waiting for you. But I can't wait....

I know what that means. You've come home early; you're lying on our bed, with your cock in your hand, your clothes strewn around the room, hurriedly discarded. For me, now the race is on. I've got to get back to you in time. Sometimes you can hold off long enough, but sometimes I'm simply too late. It's a game we play and if I get home fast enough, sex is my reward.

I text you back.

I'll be there.

I glance up at the clock; I'm contracted to sit in this chair for another fifteen minutes. I save the document I'm working on and power down my computer. Hoping no one will notice what I'm doing, I change my high heels for flats and get my bag ready to leave. My boss walks by my desk so I pretend to have my head down, reading an important paper. Thankfully he doesn't stop to talk to me.

As soon as the minute hand reaches the vertical, I'm out of my chair and pulling on my jacket.

"Night all," I call, as I hurry through the open-plan office toward the door.

Down in the parking garage I fumble with the combination lock on my bicycle. More haste, less speed—twice I get the numbers in the wrong order. But then the lock's off and I strap my bag to the rack on the back. If only I had decided to bring the car this morning, I would have had a better chance of getting to you in time. Now I'm faced with a twenty-minute cycle ride, and I don't want to be too exhausted at the other end for what you have planned.

I have to stand on the pedals to make it up the steep slope out of the office garage. I duck around the end of the barrier, waving at the security guard in his little box. Once I'm out on the street, it's a downward slope and I'm able to settle back on the saddle to catch my breath. I love this old bike, but it's hardly a racer. Several times you've offered to buy me something more aerodynamic, with a comfortable gel saddle and god knows how many gears, but I'm not interested. When I'd had this bike for a while, I christened it Barry. I've ridden miles sitting on Barry's shiny leather saddle, which has been polished to a chestnut patina by the pumping action of my buttocks. And when I'm thinking of you as I ride, the hard, slippery saddle pushing up between my legs only adds to my anticipation.

The traffic's heavy, but with the slight downward gradient I'm able to pick up speed. After seven blocks of rhythmic pumping on the pedals, I start to raise a sweat. I know the route like the back of my hand and I practically cycle on autopilot, so my thoughts turn to you, waiting for me at home. By the time I get back to the house it will be more than half an hour since you sent the text. I know you can wait that long if you want to; but sometimes you get bored and start without me. In my mind's eye I watch you slowly moving your hand up and down your cock with the lightest of touches. Your eyes are closed and you're totally relaxed as you lie there, savoring the sensations.

When this happens I try to creep into the room silently, listening to the small grunts and moans that you make as your grasp becomes firmer. It really turns me on to see you touching yourself, and I pedal even faster at the thought of it. Now I'm swooping across the sidewalk and through the park gates; there are no cars here and very few pedestrians, so I can really put my foot down on the pedals. I lift myself a little from the seat and my frantic peddling makes Barry lurch from side to side, the hard leather slapping against the inside of my thighs. I'm really flying now and the burning sensation between my legs is in direct contrast to the cold air streaming through my hair and blasting my face.

The path is flat around the lake and for several hundred yards beyond, but then I reach the steep hill that falls away to the other side of the park. As I go over the edge my speed increases; now I must stop peddling and start to use the brakes. I sit back hard on the saddle, pushing down with my hips, wondering whether I will be home in time for you. As I go even faster, I tuck forward, bending low over the handlebars. This makes Barry's saddle push farther forward between my legs. I'm wearing a skirt today that hangs around my legs and the seat, rather than being tucked up underneath me; now, through the thin silk of my panties, I can feel the hard leather tip nudging against my clit. I'm still thinking of you, waiting for me in all your naked glory. I'm thinking of what I want to do to you when I get home. I want to take your huge, rock-solid cock into my mouth and suck on it as hard as I can. For as long as it takes, though that won't be long as you've probably been playing with yourself for the last half hour. A shimmer of desire flutters through me, making me catch my breath and grip the handlebars more tightly.

At the bottom of the hill I grind my hips in a side-to-side motion as the path swerves through a series of curves. I imagine I'm riding you like I'm riding this bicycle: straddling you and guiding your cock between my legs, rising up and down as you buck and swerve underneath me. I love to be on top and you love it, too. Can you wait long enough for that? Can you hold off for something better than just your hand? I bite my bottom lip, willing you to give me just a few more moments to reach you.

I fly through the park gates, nearly flattening a woman with a buggy as I cross the sidewalk. Thinking about you and what we're going to do together is not conducive to safe cycling. The woman shouts swear words after me, but I'm long gone and I don't care. I'm on a mission to get back to you.

Now comes the hard part. The long, drawn-out hill, the last climb toward home. Trying to make the most of my momentum, my legs start pumping the pedals. Heat builds in the muscles of my thighs and buttocks, matching the fire that your text started deep within me. My panties are damp, making me slip and slide against the saddle. Each rotation of the pedals presses me from side to side. Each turn of the wheels brings me closer to home. And each grind of my hips against my bicycle deepens the need in me for you.

I'm panting with the exertion of peddling up the hill. But that's not the only thing making me pant. The sensations coursing through my body match the images in my mind. I need to reach you in time, before you reach your moment of no return. The pumping, grinding, pushing, gasping ascent is relentless. It goes on forever. I'm sweating now and tiring, but never for one minute will I consider getting off the bicycle and walking. It's simply not an option.

When I reach the top of the hill my mouth is dry and my muscles are burning. I think about kissing you, on the lips and in other places, and my mouth floods with saliva. I can quite literally taste you: the sweetness of your mouth when you've been drinking wine, the salt of perspiration on your skin, the bittersweet taste of precum on the end of your cock. I'm hungry for you. Starving. I want to devour you and I can't wait.

The road from here is straight and flat. I pedal hard enough to build up speed and then lift my feet from the spinning pedals. Flexing my hips backward and forward produces the most delicious sensation. I am so ready for you, no matter what you have in mind or what you want to do. My skirt flips up in a gust of wind and for a second I get a whiff of musk, the smell of my own anticipation. It turns me on even more, and I feel a warm rush between my legs. I'm wet, I'm sticky: I need you.

My feet find the pedals again for the final push. I fiddle with the gears to help me accelerate, though I'm already going as fast as I can. I'm nearly at the junction, the turn into the lane where we live. I pull up sharply to avoid a car that is indicating left, cursing the second that this will cost me. When my path is clear I push off again, and finally I am in our road.

A hundred yards or so, but my legs are complaining bitterly now. I am almost out of breath. But the vision of you keeps me going. We live in an old part of town, in a tiny cottage at the end of this narrow lane. Nothing has changed for a hundred years and beneath my wheels there are still cobblestones. Barry the bike judders and shudders and bumps on the uneven surface, the vibrations passing through the metal frame and the leather saddle. I sit back heavily on my seat and as the vibrations spin along my nerves and shiver through my bones, I can't pedal quite so hard. The bicycle shakes beneath me, sending tremors up my spine. Inside my mind, you are underneath me, bumping and grinding, taking me to the brink, pushing me over the edge.

Ohhhh...

I can't hold it. It's too late. I'm coming.

I stop the bike and slump forward over the handlebars as uncontrolled pleasure flashes through me. I stand there in the street and think of you as my orgasm rips through me. I gasp and hang on to the bicycle to stop myself from sinking to the ground.

I'm so sorry, babe, I didn't make it home to you. You'll be waiting and wanting on our bed, and I'll walk in sweaty and spent. It happened again. It always happens.

It's those damned cobbles.

They get me every time.

EMBRACEABLE YOU

Blair Erotica

As she slipped out of the bed, a glimpse of her smile, captured out of the corner of his eye, caught his attention. It wasn't her satisfied, what-a-night-we-had kind of smile, even if it had been that kind of night. No, this was her sneaky, crafty smile, the kind she put on when she had something devious in mind.

He ran his eyes over the lines of her body the same way he had run his hands over her earlier, in the early hours of the morning. Looking at her always made him think of the Gershwin song "Embraceable You." Well, maybe she didn't bring the song to mind, but the title for sure.

He wondered what her smile meant. What could she have in mind? Although she had a knack for coming up with delightful schemes and sexy drama, like the time she seduced him in an alley (well, he didn't make her try all that hard), this morning there wasn't time for any devilish plots. She was getting up to leave on a business trip; she had to catch some insanely early flight.

He sighed at the idea of being without her for an entire

week, the emptiness he'd feel being without her company and body. He had nothing special going on at work to fill his time; nothing in particular to throw himself into; nothing to consume the extra hours.

It would be a long week.

He imagined it would be easier for her as she would be going to London for the first time, meeting important clients and staying busy. It was easy to expect that the days and even the nights would go by quickly for her.

His best shot was to get together with some old college buddies for a poker game or something, but that didn't promise a week's worth of distraction. But that was life.

She had done her best to make certain he knew that she would miss him too—body and soul. When they came home from dinner that evening, the night before her departure, she had him sit on the couch while she fixed drinks. When she walked toward him, the movement of her hips made her slinky black dress wiggle in the most enticing way. Then she handed both glasses to him and bent down to kiss him. Before he knew what was happening, she knelt down and undid his pants, took his cock in her small hand and guided it between her moist lips. Then that devilish smile beamed up at him as she sucked his cock.

Afterward he ate her too, of course, just hiking her dress to her waist and pushing her lacy panties to one side and running his tongue into all the places that made her quiver. Sexy enough, perhaps, but it just got them both fired up.

As he recalled the evening, he remembered that those drinks were still in the living room, untouched, and he laughed.

"What are you laughing at?" she asked.

"We never drank the drinks you fixed," he said.

Her eyes glowed. "It's okay; I got enough to drink." Then she kissed him and headed into the bathroom.

They had done what they could to fill up on the joy of each other's bodies but no night was long enough for that. Still, they had made a valiant effort.

"I'm glad it's a long flight," she had said by way of weak protest early in the morning, when he tucked the front of his body against her half-asleep back and then lifted her leg so that he could press his hard cock into her cunt. "I am going to need some rest." Then, as he drove his cock into her, her eyes rolled back and her hand touched his cock where it separated her labia. "It really is good that I can sleep on the plane."

Unfortunately, he decided, lust was something that you couldn't satisfy ahead of time. It couldn't be made to work like some prepaid phone card. No matter how often or how many ways they coupled, it did nothing for the tomorrows that lay ahead. He knew he would be wanting her the moment she was gone. His brain and body worked that way.

"You can't just fuck your brains out and have the feeling stay with you long enough," he moaned. But the truth was, with her, wanting her didn't ever really stop. It amazed him that when they were together, he found himself thinking of how he wanted to take her the next time, or anticipating what she might do, even before he had even recovered from the last time he had spent inside her eager body.

Although she was as bad as he was, she teased him about it. Her teasing was erotic too, as she did it in ways that ensured he knew it flattered and pleased her that he wanted her so much, so often.

Now, hearing the water run in the shower, he thought of getting up and joining her. It was fantastic to slip into the shower and touch her slippery naked body, with shampoo streaming down over her breasts, her ass, her pussy. More than once he had wrapped his arms around her and let her feel him throbbing against her, then let her brace herself with her hands on the wet tiles of the wall, while he fucked her from behind.

This time he resisted the temptation. She had to be on time for the plane. Once he started...well, she wouldn't make it to the airport on time, not unless she told him no, and she didn't like to do that. He sighed. Her ass was so lovely, so pleasant in his hands, whether he took her from behind or put his arms around her to clutch her ass and pull her against him while she wrapped her legs around him, digging her heels into him. Thoughts of her ass made him tingle. They hadn't done anal in a while, he realized, and it suddenly seemed a significant omission.

"That is a lovely picture you've conjured up," he said out loud, feeling his cock swell. "And I doubt it will help."

When he heard the water shut off he realized it was too late to change his mind. Then the hair dryer hummed softly and he thought about how she would sit in the chair in the bathroom, with a towel wrapped around her but usually slipping down off her breasts, as she dried her hair. She kept it short, so it didn't take long, but it was sexy to watch.

She came back in the room with a towel around her, but she dropped it to the floor, smelling of soap and shampoo. As she began dressing he watched her ass and could also see her front reflected in the full-length mirror. She had set out her clothes the day before, and now she put them on slowly. It was the armor of the office: silk blouse, stockings, heels, panties, skirt. Nothing special, but as she dressed it added up to a woman that, for him, was far more than the sum of the parts.

He lazed on the bed, his cock throbbing, wondering if he could convince her to give him a blow job before she left. Of course that would just delay the inevitable getting horny again. But a delay was good, wasn't it? Better to suffer later than now.

Because she stood with her back to him, that luscious ass,

wrapped in tight cotton, was right there by his face. He reached out to put his hand between her legs. His hand touched her thigh, feeling the stockings under his fingers, and she turned her head to smile down at him with that crafty smile again. It seemed like a challenge. He moved his hand up under her skirt and she didn't protest, although she pretended to be preoccupied with buttoning her blouse. When his fingers worked their way under the elastic of her panties she fidgeted, but her legs opened a bit for him.

He heard her catch her breath when his fingers pressed the lips of her cunt open.

This, he thought, was where she had to stop him; he couldn't stop himself any longer. His fingers moved into her warm cunt, caressing the folds, hunting down her clitoris, and she bent forward slightly, putting her hands on the mirror and moaning softly as he found it.

It was gorgeous watching her reflection, her mouth opening, making a small O as his fingers teased and aroused her. He twisted on the bed to get his other hand between her legs, slipping those fingers inside the other leg of her panties to explore her vagina. She was soft and moist, and he let his fingers play with her as they would—little creatures of pleasure who lived solely to burrow into her cunt and toy with her.

And he felt her hips jerk, her vagina convulse, and he knew he had brought her off.

He freed his fingers from the tangle of cunt flesh and panties and sat up, grabbing her by the waist and putting her facedown on the bed. He tugged her skirt up to her waist and pulled her panties down around her knees, and then he straddled her legs. He grabbed her wrists and pulled her hands back to her ass.

"That ass has been calling me all morning," he said. "Show it to me," and her fingers pulled her asscheeks apart.

He sighed at the sight of her anus, and reached to the night-stand where they kept the tube of lubricant. While she held herself open to him, he squeezed it onto her anus and then pressed a fingertip on the little hole and worked it inside, loving the sensation of the tight ring. She moaned and the wiggle she gave her hips as his finger penetrated her excited him.

He finger-fucked her ass and when he felt her relaxing, he took out his finger. "Time for the grand entrance," he said lying on her and guiding his cock to her anus. He had fucked her ass before, but never liked this, with her legs held together, and it made entering her even tighter than usual. When the tip slipped inside, her anus gripping his cock as if it wanted to hold it inside, he grabbed her wrists and spread her arms out over her head. He lowered himself over her and with a jerk of his hips began taking her ass.

The sensation of his cock in her ass was incredible. Well, he liked his cock in her almost any way, and she loved to take it in every way they had tried so far. He wanted to drive deep inside her, but this way his thrusts were held a bit short. Still, it was glorious.

"You are fucking my ass while I am almost completely dressed," she hissed. "You insatiable lover."

And he knew she was loving it too.

After he came, spending himself in the tight confines of her ass, he lay on her, feeling the intensity of the moment soften into a gentle sense of well-being. He found himself thinking about fixing them a breakfast. A mimosa and, for some reason, he thought of ham sandwiches with the special ham he had brought home from the deli the day before. They would eat and then, when life came back into him, he would ask her to ride his cock....

Then he looked at her lying there, seeming to savor the sensations of the aftermath of their fuck. Her only movement since he rolled off her had been to pull her panties off and let them fall on the floor.

"Aren't you going to miss your plane?" he asked.

"No," she said.

"No?"

"I don't have to go this morning."

"But you do have to go?"

She nodded. "No way out it. Business and all that."

He ran his hands over her face, touched the lips that he loved to kiss and to have on his cock. "So when do you go?"

Her nose wrinkled. "I am not telling you."

He laughed. "So why this game?"

She rolled over and pulled his face close before kissing him. "Because it was fun. Because I knew that you wouldn't be able to resist just one more wild fuck. Because it gave us last night." She smiled. "Need any more reasons?"

He saw how she was enjoying herself. "So one of these days I'll find you've gone off to catch a plane."

She nodded. "I'll leave a note. You are the one who pointed out that there is no way we can manage to make it easy. So I need to find a way to sneak out the back way."

"I just came in the back way," he said, kissing her again.

"My point exactly," she said.

"Are you leaving today?"

"Maybe not," she said, licking her lips. "What rule says a trip should have only one great good bye?"

"You are marvelously devious as well as embraceable," he said. And he began singing, "my sweet embraceable you..." softly.

She began to undo the buttons on her blouse, watching his eyes as she bared her breasts and touched her hard nipple. "Does embraceable mean the same thing as fuckable?"

"I can accept that interpretation," he said.

She crawled on top of him, straddling his body and taking off her blouse. He laughed as she started humming the same tune that had been running through his head and then sang, "Embrace me, you insatiable you...."

FREE RIDE

Heidi Champa

For three months, I asked nearly every cabdriver I rode with if I could suck his cock. I was stoked when one finally said yes.

I don't know what possessed me to start doing it. Maybe it was the fact that I was in a brand-new city, in a brand-new country where I didn't know a soul. Maybe I was just lonely and horny. That seems most likely. Plus, it seemed like a good idea at the time.

I still hadn't gotten used to the idea of riding in the front seat of cabs. In America, we never did that, unless you were the unlucky one of the group who wouldn't fit in the back. But, in Australia, it was customary for lone male passengers to ride up front. I could never get a clear answer as to why, but who was I to buck convention?

I guess the first time I asked my driver if I could blow him, alcohol was to blame. I'd spent a night out with some guys from my university class and had no luck finding anyone interesting to take back to my apartment. I mean, flat. Actually, since I'd arrived, I'd only had two hookups. I thought being American would set me apart, but instead, it usually made me odd man out. I stumbled into the cab that night and when I looked at the driver, I thought he was hot. The Aussie accent always killed me, too. That, combined with his thick forearms, was enough to make the question pop out of my mouth after he pulled up to the curb in front of my building. He merely smiled and said he didn't swing that way. I walked to my door, dejected, and spent the rest of my waking hours beating off.

Some other cabbies weren't so kind with their replies. I'd been sworn at a lot and had many rides cut short, but on the bright side, it helped me learn the streets of my neighborhood. One guy pretended he didn't speak English so he couldn't understand my request, but he'd spoken it fine when he picked me up. Luckily for me, no one decided that the only way to respond to my question was with a swift punch to the face, although a few looked as if they wanted to.

When I got into the cab that fateful night, I took one look at the driver and wasn't even going to ask. His gruff expression and the angry growl in his voice when he asked me where I was headed made me think twice. My streak looked like it was going to come to an end, obviously not counting the ladies who'd picked me up along the way. But after I told him where I was going, my mind started to change. It had been a long week. Finals at university had kicked my ass and I was keyed up and looking for some release. As the driver twisted and turned through the streets that led me home, I kept looking at him out of the corner of my eye.

"Something you wanna say, buddy?"

His question surprised me, and at first I only shook my head.

"Because it seems like you got something on your mind."

"It does?"

"Well, you keep looking over here. Gotta problem?"

"No, I don't. Sorry."

He started laughing and slapped me on the shoulder.

"No worries, mate. I just find it helps weed out the creeps if I ask up front. Usually keeps them quiet the rest of the trip. But, you don't look like a creep."

"Good to know."

He slammed on his breaks as a car stopped short in front of us, and cursed under his breath.

"Jesus, this has been a shit of a night. Thankfully, you're my last pickup. I can't wait to get to the pub."

I opened my mouth to say something, but was cut off by the blare of his car horn, his anger bubbling up again at the cars in front of us.

"Goddamn this city is full of morons."

I cleared my throat and tried to make polite conversation.

"It must suck to be a cabdriver."

He chuckled before flipping on his turn signal, which I noticed was on the opposite side of the wheel than I was used to.

"You could say that. But it does have the occasional perk."

He turned to look at me as we drifted to a stop at a red light.

"Yeah? What's that?" I asked, his eyes still locked on me.

"You wouldn't believe me if I told you."

"Try me."

He smiled and shook his head as we started moving again, his strong hands turning the wheel with ease.

"Let's just say that every now and then I get a very generous customer."

"You mean a good tipper? Because I didn't think tipping was all that common in Australia."

"Something like that."

The car turned onto my street and stopped in front of my building. He turned the meter off and jotted down something in a notebook on the console.

"That'll be seven dollars fifty."

I pulled out my wallet, ready to pay and go, without asking the question I was dying to ask. The ten dollars in my hand went right back in between the other bills when I looked into his eyes. Hey, we'd both had a bad day, right?

"Can I suck your cock?"

His eyes widened in shock, but he soon was grinning.

"What did you say?"

I swallowed hard and repeated myself.

"Can I suck your cock?"

"Why would you wanna do something like that?"

"Does it really matter why?"

He shifted in his seat and rubbed his hands over his thighs. I waited for him to kick me out of the car, but instead he grabbed a handful of my shirt and pulled me into a kiss.

"Not to me, mate."

I took off my seat belt and leaned toward him, but he pushed me back.

"Not here."

He took off down the street and after a few quick turns, we were in a lonely alley, the only lights the ones coming from the dashboard.

"Get in the back, mate."

I pushed the door open and stepped out into the night air. There was a moment I thought about running away, forgetting the whole thing. But I couldn't. I'd come this far. I'd asked for a reason. When I slipped into the backseat, I heard his belt buckle jingling and the metallic click of his zipper going down. In the dim light of the cab, I saw his hand wrap around his cock and start stroking. Without a word, I leaned over and pushed his fist aside, wrapping my lips around the fat head of his cock. His hand went to my hair immediately, twining in the strands and giving a slight tug right before he pushed himself deeper into my throat. The sound of his groans filled the quiet of the cab, along with the creaking of the vinyl seat underneath us.

Normally I didn't like guys who were so forceful, but with the cabbie, it only served to make me hotter and harder. My cock was straining against the zipper of my jeans and I couldn't stand it anymore. I opened my pants with my free hand and fished out my dick, wrapping my hand around it to try to ease the ache. When his hand relaxed a bit, I took back a bit of control and my tongue traced the length of his shaft. I paused at the tip and swirled my tongue all the way around before sucking the tip back between my lips.

"Fuck, that feels good, mate."

In the distance, I could hear traffic on the main street, the sound of blaring horns and squealing brakes. The cabbie slouched farther down the seat and started pushing his hips up, thrusting his cock even deeper. His iron grip was back as well and all I could do was take it as he fucked my mouth, the force making me gag a few times, but I didn't care. My hand kept working my own cock, but most of my attention was focused on the stranger who had finally fulfilled my misguided fantasy.

His moans had turned to grunts, and I could feel the muscles in his legs flexing with effort. When he started to move faster, I did my best to keep up with him, but it was mostly a lost cause. With a loud roar, he started coming, his hot load hitting the back of my throat so I had no choice but to swallow him down. I felt him relax, bit by bit, until the tension that had filled his body since I'd climbed into the cab was completely gone. I gave the head of his cock one last lick before I sat up. I wiped my mouth on my sleeve in the dark and had started to close my pants when he stopped me.

"Hey, I can't let you go home with blue balls, mate."

He yanked my pants and boxers down to my knees and wrapped a meaty fist around my cock.

"You don't have to do that."

I don't know why I protested, but thankfully for me, he didn't listen.

"I know."

I could just make out his smile in the dark before he lowered his head and I felt his tongue swipe over the head of my cock. I gasped before I could stop it, the feeling overwhelming. It had been way too long since I'd been with anyone and within a few minutes he had me dangerously close to the edge. Trying to slow him down seemed useless; his pace only increased as he took me deeper. My toes curled in my shoes and I tried to think about my physics test or composition class, anything to keep me from coming too soon.

It took all my strength to push him away, just so I could have a moment to breathe.

"Something wrong?" he asked, his hand replacing his mouth around my dick.

I sighed at the continued contact and had to close my eyes.

"I'm too close. I didn't want it to be over yet."

"Well, all you had to do was say so, mate."

I expected him to stop; instead his mouth was back on me in an instant, but this time, the intensity was replaced by the light tease of his tongue. He licked every inch of me before taking one of my balls in his mouth, then the other. I gripped the seat for dear life when he started sucking my cock again, his pace starting slow and increasing with each bob of his head. This time, I didn't stop him when I felt myself losing control. But I felt like I should warn him.

"Oh god. I'm gonna come."

I bit my lip to stop myself from yelling, but it was no use. My hips started to lift off the seat as if I had no control over them, my body wracked with spasms as I came into his mouth. The cab got quiet as we pulled apart and as exhausted as I was, I managed to pull up my pants. He got out of the backseat and back behind the wheel and I followed his lead. Without a word, he started the car and within minutes, we were back in front of my apartment complex. I pulled out my wallet to pay the fare, but he stopped me.

"Keep your money, mate."

"You sure? What about the pub?"

"I think I've got it covered. Besides, you turned my day right around."

I turned to open the door, but he pulled me back, kissing me hard.

"So, is this what you meant by perks of the job?" I asked.

"Yeah, I'd have to say it qualifies." He jammed a business card into my hand and leaned back, smiling as he spoke.

"Next time you need a ride, mate, give me a call."

"I will."

"Tell me something, how many other drivers have you asked?"

I smiled and lied through my teeth.

"You're the first."

WHEN HE GETS HOME

Lucy Felthouse

The moment Nina heard the rumble of her husband's car engine as he pulled into the drive, she dropped her book and all but leapt out of her chair. Moving fast across the living room, then through the kitchen, she flung open the internal door that led into the garage. Walking in, she closed it behind her. Standing, arms folded, one foot tapping repeatedly on the floor, she waited for Owen to drive the car into the garage, then press the button that shut the door behind him and the vehicle. When the bottom of the up-and-over touched concrete and the car's ignition was shut off, she practically ran around to the driver's side and tugged the door open before Owen got the chance.

The sight of his wife standing there, an indeterminable expression on her face, made Owen's heart sink. He had no idea what was going on, and she never normally came into the garage to meet him when he got home. She didn't look very happy, either. He didn't speak, as he suspected whatever he said would be the wrong thing.

Nina didn't speak, either. There were no words to explain what she was thinking and feeling right now, so she decided that instead of talking, she'd just act. That decided, she leaned forward and touched the button to recline the seat Owen was sitting in. She smirked at his expression—the poor man had no idea what was coming to him. She was going to make sure he'd never forget it, either.

Owen's body jerked as he responded to the shock of the back support disappearing from behind him. Nina's expression still looked strange—yet eerily beautiful—and when she rested a palm on his chest and shoved him, he landed on the now-flat backrest with a thump that knocked the air out of his lungs. "W-what are you—?" His hastily spoken words were cut off when Nina straddled his lap and silenced him by leaning down and pressing her lips to his.

Nina couldn't help but find Owen's reaction amusing. He looked as though he thought she was going to kill him or something. Despite that, she felt his cock hardening beneath her and was glad her husband's body was ready, even if his brain couldn't quite catch up. She knelt up enough so she could slide her hand between their bodies and cup his crotch, squeezing and stroking his rapidly growing erection.

Owen's eyes widened as his wife played with his hard-on through his suit trousers, then abruptly tugged down his fly, slipped her hand through the gap and maneuvred his cock out through it. Part of him wanted to say something about the fact that the edges of the zip might scratch his shaft, possibly even draw blood, but the rest of him said to shut up—he was about to get laid. In the car, no less!

Enjoying the feeling of warm velvet over a core of steel in her hand, Nina wrapped her fingers more tightly around Owen's cock and began to stroke it slowly, ensuring he was fully erect before moving so her hips rested over his. She tucked the material of her skirt to one side, revealing her knickerless lady parts. Then, aiming the head of his prick at her entrance, she slowly lowered herself onto him, her damp pussy growing rapidly wetter at the excitement and danger of what they were doing.

Owen let out a moan as the wet warmth of his wife's cunt sunk down onto his cock. The saucy wench had come out here with no knickers on, set on seducing him! She clapped her hand over his mouth quickly, muffling the sound. She put a finger of her other hand to her lips, then pointed upward. *Ahh, the kids were in.* He nodded in understanding, and she released him.

Wordlessly, Nina began to bounce up and down on his dick, lifting herself so he almost popped out of her, leaving just the very tip of him inside, then dropping down heavily. It wasn't a particularly fast movement, but it was packed full of friction and she knew that if she carried on like that, it wouldn't be long before Owen shot his load. Desperate to ensure she got her rocks off, too, she grabbed one of his hands from around her waist and thrust it to her crotch. Mercifully, he got the hint and, gathering some juices from where their bodies joined, he smeared them over her swollen clit and started to stroke.

Owen's actions had a knock-on effect. Touching his wife's nub caused her eyes to roll back in her head and her pussy to contract around his cock, which in turn caused his cock to throb and twitch inside her. He'd have to up his game if he wanted to make sure she came before—or at the same time as—him. Grasping the slippery and sensitive bundle of nerve endings between his finger and thumb, he rolled and pinched at it. Amazingly, it swelled further at his ministrations, and he looked up to see Nina stifling her own moans by biting down on her fist.

Nina knew it wouldn't be long now for either of them. The

setting and situation were unusual, forbidden and quite kinky, particularly for her and her husband. She was sure other couples had sex in all kinds of weird and wonderful places, but she and Owen were very much missionary-in-bed kind of people. Judging by the way they were both reacting to the impromptu fuck in the garage, though, that was set to change. Her pussy fluttered around Owen's shaft, and the tightening in her abdomen, like a spring wound tighter and tighter, told her just how imminent her climax was. "You close?" she breathed.

Owen nodded, glad that Nina was almost ready to come, as he knew there was no way he could hold on for much longer. He wished he could see all of her gorgeous body as she bounced up and down on his shaft, her perfect tits and ass, her curves in all the right places...but it wasn't the time or the place. Maybe later. Right now, though, the tingle at the base of his spine and the tightening of his balls told him he was approaching the point of no return. He stimulated Nina's clit faster and harder, seeking the particular spot that never failed to send her over the edge. The twitches around his shaft indicated he'd found it. He focused hard there as Nina rode them both to completion.

Nina dug her teeth harder into her hand, her eyes widening as Owen manipulated the most sensitive spot, just at the edge of her clitoral hood. He knew it drove her crazy and clearly intended to take advantage of that fact. Soon, the sensation in her abdomen was at a breaking point and she removed her fingers from her mouth just in time to whisper, "Now."

Owen let go, the spunk making its journey from his balls, up his shaft and out of his slit in what seemed like record time. He gripped Nina's hips hard—harder than he meant to—and squeezed his eyes and mouth closed in an attempt not to shout out as the intense sensations of climax crashed through every last cell of his body. He couldn't prevent the odd humming noise he made, but nobody but Nina would have been able to hear it in any case.

Nina slumped down onto Owen's prone form, her cunt still twitching wildly around his shaft as she rode out the waves of her pleasure. They smashed into her, again and again, wringing her out, turning her world upside down in the most perfect, blissful way. It seemed like an age since she'd had an orgasm like that, and she suspected that come bedtime, she'd be eager for another one.

They lay panting together for a few moments more, until finally Owen cupped his wife's face in his hands and gave her a long, lingering kiss. He pulled away earlier than he really wanted to, aware that if he carried on much longer, they'd both end up ready and raring to go again, and they were already running the risk of being caught. "Baby," he said, stroking Nina's hair, "as much as I'd love to lie here all night with you, and definitely fuck you again, do you think we ought to go inside?"

Nina sighed. "I suppose so. Ugh."

They reluctantly made themselves decent, clambered out of the car and headed into the house. Owen, more out habit than any need for security, pressed the button on his key fob to lock the car, before closing the door to the garage.

"So," Nina said as innocently as possible to her husband, having spotted the kids entering the kitchen, "how was your trip, darling? Glad to have you home."

"It was fine, sweetheart, thank you. But I couldn't have wished for a better homecoming. Hi, kids!"

BEFORE
THEY BURN

Beatrix Ellroy

I hadn't meant to gasp, biting off a moan, when Aral slapped me on the ass. But I had.

In all fairness, he had started it, reaching out to steal a cookie from the cooling rack; I'd absentmindedly slapped his hand, still holding the piping bag with my other. But instead of drawing his hand back, like any naughty boy caught with his hand in the cookie jar, he'd grabbed my wrist.

He still held it firmly, his fingers circling completely around my wrist like a cuff. When I looked up at him he grinned, crooked and full of challenge, then slapped me on the ass. One big open-handed swat, right on my asscheek. He was looking right at me as he did it, could not have missed the gasp, or the soft moan bitten off as I closed my mouth.

His smile was broad, but his eyes were dark in the fading light. I snatched my hand back and continued piping the cookies onto the tray, looking down, cursing the blush I knew was rising on my cheeks, the tips of my ears and probably the bare skin above the low back of my shirt. I usually loved the way it felt, my hair brushing my skin, but I suddenly felt naked, exposed. He disappeared for a moment, and I let go the breath I didn't realize I'd been holding.

I ignored the slight trembling in my hands and went back to piping. Guests would be arriving soon and I loved the smell of fresh cookies, the delicate crumble against my tongue. And since it was my birthday, I was going to give myself that small pleasure. And the smell of freshly baked deliciousness always added a little something special to the party, so I usually timed the cooking fairly close. Even so, Aral shouldn't even have been here, but his plane had arrived late so he'd come straight here instead of the hotel. There was a strange and not unwelcome intimacy to being alone with him in my kitchen, in my house.

In truth I barely knew him, had only met him once or twice at other parties, at friends' houses as he traveled through for work. He had always caught my eye, with his dark hair wild and curling, his skin the color of good caramel and the most wicked smile. So he was a distraction, even before his hand came down on my ass.

When I heard the dull tread of his boots on the tiled floor again I bowed my head farther, willing my body back under control. He came to stand behind me, crowding against me. I looked down and could see his boots, heavy and black, huge beside my bare feet. His breath was on the back of my neck and I felt a shiver rising, felt my breath quicken, my heart hammer. The cookies I piped became erratic as he simply stood behind me, saying nothing. I finished the tray, then stopped. He laughed knowingly, then stepped back, making enough room for me to pull the oven door open without burning myself but not enough to stop my ass pressing against him as I leaned down. I bit down on my tongue and concentrated on sliding the baking tray onto the oven rack, trying to ignore the press of his legs against mine, the hardness of his muscular thighs.

I shut the oven door with a slam, and then spun to face him, pressing back against the bench, feeling the heat from the oven rise against my thighs. He smiled, with his hands curled loosely at his sides; he spread them out, as if in question, and I couldn't look away from the breadth of them, the promise of power in their size. I said the first thing that came to mind.

"I need to get these out in ten minutes."

He grinned wickedly and stepped forward again. "Then I'll have to be quick." He reached past me and turned the timer dial. "We both know I heard that little gasp—that little moan." He put his hands either side of me, leaning over with his face close to mine. "I aim to make you moan again, Orya."

He caught my lips in a kiss, soft and wet, oddly gentle. We stood like that, kissing, with the heat rising around us, for a long moment. I could feel the tension building, and my hands clenched uselessly on the bench. He moved his own hands to cover them, hold them still, and I moaned into his mouth as I felt the press of his fingers against my wrists.

"Ah, there it is, my sweetness." He spoke with his face close to me, lips brushing mine. "It takes a little bit of roughness, does it? A little bit of domination?" I blushed again as I pulled against his grip. He pulled my hands behind my back and caught them together with one of his own, holding my face still with the other. "Say it. Say it, Orya, or I stop." There was no smile on his face now, his eyes solidly black in the midafternoon light. He kissed me again, harsh and vicious, and I moaned into his mouth; he pulled back, pulled away and I met his eyes.

"Yes," I breathed.

"Yes what? Say it properly." His voice was low and dark, almost a growl.

"Yes, I need roughness. Yes, I need your hands on me."

He smiled then, crooked and sly. "Good." He pulled me forward, my hands still clamped together at the small of my back, and then he bent me over the counter and let go of my hands.

"I want you to stay still, hands flat." He finally pressed himself against me, positioning my hands beside my shoulders, his cock a hard line against my soft flesh. I moaned and wriggled my ass against him, lifting to my toes to try to press my quim against the hardness. He laughed again and stepped back, landing a hard swat on my ass. "I said stay still." He swatted my other cheek. "I want you to moan, make noise, but do not move."

I swallowed and dropped my heels to the floor, ready to be still. He made a sharp noise. "I said, *still*." He cupped his hand between my legs, lifting me to my toes again, and my hands spasmed, reaching out to brace myself, to hold on to something. He made the noise again and repositioned my hands, then placed his own broad palm on the center of my back.

"If you move once more, it won't just be your ass that I spank."

My legs quivered and I could feel my knickers soak. He slapped my ass again, hard, and I let out a low moan. Swiftly he spanked me, first one cheek then the other. I fought to stay still, my calves and thighs aching, my fingertips pressed tightly to the wooden bench beneath me. Embarrassingly quickly I began to beg, the swift swat of his hand on my ass and the careless strength of the hand pinning me to the counter combining to make me wet and quivering, desperate.

"Please, please." I almost sobbed.

He stopped spanking and gently stroked my ass over my jeans. "Please what?"

"Please Aral, I want to, I need to come." I couldn't hold the position anymore and let my heels drop, let my body rest on the counter. He leaned down and looped his arm through mine, holding it tight with his hand, broad and warm on the back of my neck, pressing my cheek against the cool wood.

"You moved." He nudged my legs apart, not gently but still mindful of my bare feet. He placed his hand over my mouth, cupping it gently. "Three slaps for that. Since you did so well at first. Three slaps, then we'll see about letting you come."

I shuddered in his grip, fear sparking along my veins. I braced myself, but he simply stroked me through my jeans for a moment, unbearably lightly. I could hear the ticking of the timer over everything, relentless. I closed my eyes, squeezing them shut. He leaned down, mouth against my ear, crushing my body into the wood.

"Count them."

He straightened, then his hand rose and fell and I choked out a moan. The tips of his fingers landed over my aching clit and I felt a spasm run through me.

"One," I gasped.

His hand rose and fell, harder this time and I fought to stay still, to not rise to my toes again.

"Two," I whimpered.

"Brace yourself."

I swallowed and squeezed my eyes shut, pressed myself into the wood. His hand rose and fell, the same weight and swing as he'd used on my ass.

"Three," I sobbed.

"Good." He let go of my neck and buried his hand in my hair, then hauled me upright, pulling my head back; my arm still looped through his forced me into a graceful arc. "Very good." He bit my neck and reached down to undo my jeans, my legs still spread wide by his booted feet. "You may come after all...as long as it's before the timer runs out."

He dipped his fingers beneath the softness of my belly, beneath my underwear. My breath came in shuddering sobs, erratic moans. When he pushed his fingers into my soaked quim I keened, high and loud. "Yes, fuck Orya, that's it." Aral's voice was rough. "Just like that. God you're wet." My hips jerked uncontrollably as he circled my clit with one finger. He bit my neck again. "Moan for me, Orya, come for me." He plunged two fingers into me, pressing the base of his thumb against my clit, and I arched up, thighs spasming, clenching around his fingers.

I moaned his name, high and loud, as I came.

He drew his fingers out of my jeans, stroking along my clit, and I spasmed against him again. With my head still pulled back he ran one of his fingers over my lips. He let go of my hair and turned me to face him, as he licked my wetness from his hand. When he was finished he spoke.

"Your cookies should be ready."

I could hear a car pulling up, doors slamming as someone else arrived. He brushed his damp fingers against my lips again, then pulled me into a vicious kiss. I heard the first guest call my name and he let me go and went to meet them, leaving me trembling and spent in the middle of the kitchen. The timer buzzed, loud and harsh, prompting me to move.

I wondered when he would come to take his own pleasure and shivered at the thought.

Throughout the night I would look over at him and he would smile, run his fingers over his lips, wink at me. Each time my heart would skip a beat and my thighs quiver. The anticipation was electric, making the hairs on the nape of my neck stand on end. I began to avoid the kitchen; each time I entered I could feel myself soak and swell again, the memory making me squirm.

After my third drink I put my glass down on the table and walked to the bathroom, smiling brightly at my friends as I passed. I couldn't see Aral, and I breathed deeply, not sure if I was disappointed or relieved.

My quim ached and when I pushed my jeans down I saw that I hadn't just soaked my knickers, but even my jeans were damp. Not enough to totally embarrass myself, but enough that I felt that blush rising again. I turned and flushed, then washed my hands. The water ran cool over my fingers and I heard the click of the lock disengaging on the door; my head flew up and in the mirror I saw Aral slide through the door and shut it behind him, locking it, and putting a sliver of metal back into his pocket.

"My turn." His eyes locked with mine in the mirror. He came to stand behind me, hands stroking up my waist to my breasts. "I want to fuck you, Orya."

I felt my breath stutter. "I don't have protection."

He smiled at me in the mirror. "After that first swat on your ass, I went and got mine." He bit down on my neck. "I knew what I wanted to do. I've known that from the first moment I met you, but it never seemed like the right time. Or place."

"But the kitchen and the bathroom, at a party, are the right time and place?" My voice was breathy, too high.

"No, but I couldn't pass up that little moan, that little gasp." His hand moved beneath my shirt, pulling at my nipples through the thin fabric of my bra. "And I can't wait for all these people to leave. Not knowing how wet you are, how fucking responsive you are." His hand clenched on my hip, on my breast, and I moaned. "Just like that. Fuck."

He began to undo my jeans again, pushing them over my ass. "Hold on to the counter," he murmured. He spanked my bare ass a few times, then pulled the condom from his pocket and opened it with his teeth. "Bend over more, Orya." I heard him undo his zip and watched in the mirror as he pulled his cock through the opening, his jeans blue against the dark skin and hair, his hand fisted around himself.

I leaned over the sink, bending over my arms, legs held together by my jeans; as Aral rolled the condom over his hard cock he ran his hand over my ass, then slipped his thumb inside my quim.

"Still so fucking wet." He landed a swat on my ass. "Up on your toes again."

I pushed up to my toes and felt his hands grab my ass, kneading it, spreading me wide, then the first touch of his cock, huge against the slickness of my quim. I let out a soft moan as he pushed in, his cock hard and thick, sliding into me. His fingers clenched hard, and I knew I would have bruises.

"Fuck. Fuck." Aral's voice was raw, rough. "Touch yourself, Orya, I want to see you make yourself come." His eyes were still locked on mine in the mirror. "I want to see your face when you come while I fuck you."

He withdrew and snapped his hips forward and I closed my eyes, moaning, then pushed one hand between my legs. At the first touch on my clit I dropped my head to rest on my other arm. Aral growled and pulled my head up by my hair.

"No, keep your head up, your eyes open. I want to see you come apart." He thrust again, pushing me forward onto my fingers. I moaned, mouth open, red and wanting. Aral snarled. "That's it. Fuck. I can't, I can't wait any longer." He let go of my hair and grabbed my hips, slamming into me over and over. I rode my own fingers, trying to keep my eyes open, watching Aral's face as he thrust. His hips hammered into me, shoving my hips against the sink. I bit down on my lips, my tongue, trying to be quiet, the sounds of the party filtering through the open window, the door, a murmur of noise beneath the sound of his flesh slamming into mine. He watched me and I watched him and I felt the burn rising from my feet and up my trembling thighs to burst between my legs; I curled up and he hissed, low, then wrenched my head up by my hair again.

"I want to watch you." He punctuated each word with a vicious thrust, my quim clenching and gripping him as I whimpered through my orgasm. The tremble sent him over the edge and I watched as he came, snarling through his teeth, fierce and beautiful in the harsh light.

He let go of my hair, lazily thrusting a few times before he pulled out, spanking me once then tying the condom in a knot and dropping it into the trash. I pushed myself upright and pulled my jeans over my slightly stinging ass; Aral tucked himself back into his pants and did them up, then pressed himself against my back, nuzzling my neck as he zipped my pants back up and buttoned them.

"Next time, Orya? I *will* take my time with you." He turned me around and caught my lips in a kiss, then lifted my still-damp fingers to his mouth, sucking gently at the tips. I shivered. He slapped my ass and turned away; I unlocked the door and slipped back into the party, the sting of his hand on my ass tingling.

WON'T LAST
THE WEEK

Preston Avery

Sunday

I meet her at a barbecue. We discover that we are friends of friends or maybe neighbors of friends of friends, or it could be friends of neighbors' friends. I am struck stupid by lust the second I see her. The moment is one that I am familiar with, but the intensity makes it different. I can't tell you what she likes to drink or what she does for a living. The problem is I don't remember *those* details, but I can tell you that we both like the old Dashboard Confessional albums and that I must have her. Regardless of, well, anything. When I approach her she smiles at me like she has been waiting for me her whole life. She lights up from the inside, just because I am there. I think maybe that's where the intensity comes in. I make my play for her just like I have made these plays before, but this isn't preseason or even the playoffs. Here and now, I'm going for a title.

We spend the night on the beach and though we talk, sharing certain little bits and pieces of ourselves, the conversation isn't what holds me. It's the magnetic pull of her body and her mouth. I don't want her to use it for speaking anymore. And then as if she knows the exact direction of my thoughts, she's done talking too. We taste each other, making sounds that are not words but older than time. Hunger fuels me. Like I haven't eaten in weeks and she is a perfectly prepared rib eye. I know I probably shouldn't liken her to a piece of meat, but for a carnivore like me, that is the ultimate compliment. A really good steak compares to little else, and she is making me lose my taste for anything but her.

She isn't skinny like the girls I usually go for, like my ideal "on paper" woman, but curved and soft and she fits me just right. Her breasts are big with a delicious slope to them, and I know they will overflow my grasp. I could bury my face in the valley between them and never come up for air. I could have seconds and thirds and fourths of her and die a gluttonous happy man. She does everything I lead her into. I don't ask—words are still lost to us. The first time I lower my hand to one of those gorgeous mounds, hidden beneath a thin blue cotton shirt, she doesn't protest or push me away—she arches into me, into my touch, and makes the most beautiful noise in her throat. That moment, those moments, are all that I can feel. The future is as unreal to me as a unicorn on the planet Saturn. That place where names and phone numbers matter is at least a world away.

Monday

I wake up before the alarm, still sandy and sticky from her. After finally getting home, I hadn't showered, refusing to rinse away that last tactile reminder. I hope that she still smells like me, covered in my sweat and saliva and semen. I spend a long time staring at the ceiling. I lick my lips and call to mind the texture of her pebbled nipples, the taste of her swollen, beer-rinsed pussy after she had stretched and flexed around me. I am hard but can't even bring myself to move, sure that will break the spell of my reverie. It's a weird sort of paralysis. Wanting to fuck my hand but knowing that stroking my dick will be a shadow of what I am imagining, what I am remembering. So I just stare at the dingy white above me until my erection subsides a little, until my alarm goes off and I have to shower because I need a paycheck and people need their packages.

Tuesday
I wish I had never met her. Especially now at 3:18 a.m., when the last thing I should be doing is ceiling gazing. I wake up with my cock like stone and my dreams suffused with her scent. I wish I could identify that smell. If she smelled like citrus and I could eat an orange, maybe I could get my head clear. Clearer at least. I can't place it, though. Or straighten any of it out.

She smells like summer, like sweet salt sweat and something that blooms, like the ocean and the sun. I have only seen her in sixty-watt fluorescents and slightly waning moonlight, and I actually have no idea what the sun smells like, but I bet it smells like her. Just pulsing and hot.

This morning the touch of my own hand isn't seeming so uncalled for. An unworthy substitute, yes, for the soft, moist clutch of her cunt, or her mouth—but sleep will be impossible until my wayward appendage is at least appeased. And so I do what I must, and take myself into my rough palm. My hand doesn't feel anything like hers, but I know exactly what to do and so it works in the way Ramen noodles can still fill you up and taste okay. One hand tugs while the other cups my balls, pulsing my index finger very slightly into my asshole. Jesus, what a gorgeous sensation when she did that to me. The memory pushes me over and once I shoot on my chest and stomach, I pause for breath and rub the come into my skin in lazy circles, feeling momentarily less urgent but still lacking.

I know the planes of my body well but feel oddly detached from my own touch, remembering how filled up my hands were when I rubbed it into her. I bring a thumb to my mouth and run my tongue over it. I had never tasted my own semen before that night, never been compelled to, but my mind is making the same lazy circles my hands were a moment ago, reminding me of when three of my fingers had been inside of her, how she brought them to her mouth and the sound she made as she sucked.

I think about how I lifted her skirt and rubbed handfuls of wet sand over her upper thighs as she shuddered too. About how by the time I poured my warm beer over the swollen satin folds of her sex and the revitalized length of my dick to rinse away the sand, by the time I was finally inside of her, we were gritty and dirty and so hot for each other that nothing else mattered. I jack off again and fall back into restless dreams of summer sun and warm welcoming skin.

Wednesday
My sleep is no better, but now my work is beginning to suffer. Also, I am surprised there is any skin left on my palm—or my penis for that matter. I am an hour and a half behind schedule and almost deliver three separate packages to the wrong addresses. Thank god I catch the mistakes before driving off.

The strange thing is I'm not just thinking about the fucking anymore. Don't get me wrong, there is still plenty of that carnality roiling around up top, but I find myself also pondering the fate of our meeting. I haven't been able to track her down, even after more phone calls than I am willing to admit. I am not even sure if I am describing her well. If I could tell any of my friends or friends of neighbors or neighbors of friends about the perfect roundness and dusky pink of her nipples or the rippling sheath of her vagina, I could distinguish her from all the other pretty girls with blue eyes and a long brown ponytail.

Foolishly I want to make them understand, to tell them how open she was to me, to every whim or manipulation I coaxed her body into, every thought in my head met with instant compliance, with greedy acceptance, with a matching hunger all her own. I am achingly aware of the difference between want and need now.

Thursday
Sleep is impossible. I am experiencing a masturbation fatigue that I don't remember being a problem in my teens, which was the last time I had spent so much time with my tool in my hand. I can't jerk off after, well, jerking off and off and off. I just stare and stare and stare instead. I see the ceiling, but I also see the vast open nothingness of the rest of my life without ever finding her.

I have the day off so there is a lot of staring happening. My mom calls and that conversation will forever be confined to the far reaches of the 90 percent of gray matter I don't use because all I could think about was slickness and sweat and sand and the scent of the sun. It reminds me, though, how she told me that night on the beach that she was raised by a single mom too, and now instead of hapless despondency, I am beginning to feel something like panic.

I am wondering what she is doing at this moment. I am wondering what she looked like when she graduated high school, and what she does for a living. Because now I am not just thinking about her body, about wrapping my prick in her long brown hair or sliding it between her breasts or inside, *god*, inside of her—any way inside, all the ways I can put my body into hers. Now I am needing to know who she is too. I am listening to *Swiss Army Romance* nonstop.

Friday
I am obsessed; I am questioning my sanity. No sleep, or if there are small snatches of it, nothing restful. I can't eat now either. Screw steak, just give me her. I would happily sacrifice food forever for just one more taste, hell, just one more glimpse of her. What have I become?

I am step-step-stepping my way door to door and leaving packages of this and packages of that but my mind is trapped in that same spiral of images and memories and imaginings of her.

That's when the proverbial "it" happens, when I find my unicorn on the planet Saturn, the gift that fate never actually bestows upon anyone in real life. I climb the stairs to apartment 16F of Fairfield Place and she opens the door in a loose white T-shirt and some type of plaid pajama pants.

"You," she says, looking breathless and a little strung out, and also like the most brilliant thing I have ever set eyes on. I hold the lightweight brown cardboard box out to her, and she steps back and opens the door wider.

She is against the wall of her tiny entry before the door has swung shut, and the first thing I do is press my nose hard into the pulse of her throat. I want to actually eat her, ingest her into myself. I am incoherent but try to speak anyway, try to tell her that I need her and have been crazy since we met, but she just shakes her head and kisses me with answering ardor. The clack of our teeth, the simultaneous urgent sounds we make when she presses her tits frantically into me, our shared rapid breathing, they are a symphony of relief. So close, so close. She is right here and I almost can't believe it. I tug her shirt up and over her head, pulling the rubber band from her hair and groaning deep when I can take those hard pink nipples in my hands again. Somehow, I remember my idling truck in the parking lot and try to break free. It's like trying to pry electromagnets apart.

"I'll be right back, right fucking back, I promise," I tell her, but she shakes her head no.

"Quickly," she counters, unbuttoning my shorts and sliding them down with my boxers as I yank at her pants. The next second I have her pinned against the wall again with my cock inside her and this artless coupling is better than my memories or anything my imagination had conjured. I feel like weeping with the sheer satisfaction of having found her. She is grabbing me in rough handfuls as I pump, pump, pump. Her vagina is tight but slick, and she is bucking against me as best she can without losing her footing. In a deft motion that I probably could never again duplicate, I move her to the patchy vinyl tile floor, on her hands and knees, and shove back into her. I want her to really, really feel me. I want to reach as deep as possible. I would worry about our knees except I know that I won't last very long.

I seize the mass of her hair right at the scalp, pulling her head back so that I can lick her sweat-dampened neck, then reach around with my other hand to pinch her clit, distended from its little hood. I am overcome with the smell of sun. It seems to burst around us, radiating as she cries out her release and I flood her pussy in jerky snaps of my hips. Before letting go, I growl into her ear, "I'm not even close to done with you."

"Good," she manages to murmur as she collapses to the floor in a panting puddle of perfection.

MELANIE'S CHOICE

Medea Mor

Thirty lashes. That's what she'd get if Steve caught her in the act. Thirty lashes with an implement of his choice, or fifty if she didn't tell him and he found out anyway.

Not that Melanie cared. She'd been horny all day. In the morning, she had woken up with her hand between her thighs, stroking herself without even being aware of it. At work, she'd found herself pressing a highlighter between her legs while drawing up her report, squeezing her thigh muscles around it as if it were a cock ready to invade. Neither action had given her any relief. Nor had it been supposed to, because she didn't have Steve's permission to come, not without him present.

They had rules, he and she. Many rules, the most important one being that Melanie wasn't allowed to orgasm unless Steve had given her permission to do so. Her orgasms belonged to him, he'd informed her when she had first moved in with him, and seeing as he tended to be generous with them, she seldom felt the need to disobey him.

Today was an exception, though. Fourteen days without Steve had sorely tested her self-control. Sitting alone on their sofa every night, Melanie had realized just how vital his presence was to her well-being, how lost and restless she felt without him there to add structure to her life and push her buttons.

As his two weeks' absence had drawn to a close, she'd grown impatient for his return, and now that it was imminent, the anticipation was positively killing her. And so it was that, when she'd gotten home that night and changed into the skimpy schoolgirl uniform he'd told her to wear on the evening of his return (*sans* underwear, naturally), she'd found herself gravitating to the black box under the TV, which was innocently labeled DVDs but really contained the majority of their not-inconsiderable collection of naughty toys.

She'd resisted the urge at first. She'd told herself that she could hold out a few more hours, until he stepped through the door and had his wicked way with her. She'd told herself that he wouldn't have kept her on edge for so long unless he was planning something special upon his return, something that would make the long wait worthwhile. But it was no use. She needed the release, and she needed it *now*.

As she rummaged through the toy box, which contained a sizable collection of punishment implements as well the requisite plugs, cuffs and vibrators, Melanie found herself wondering what thirty lashes of each implement would feel like on her near-naked backside in the event that Steve should walk in on her while she was pleasuring herself. She knew from experience that the oiled leather flogger would leave quite a nasty sting. So would the small black flogger with the knots on the ends of the falls. Thirty swats with that and she'd probably regret her impatience. Yet part of her *hoped* he'd catch her in the act, just to experience the intensity of a flogging or spanking again. She craved the pain, the ritual of submitting to him for punishment. She needed him to take control of her, to bring her to heel when her frustration led her to challenge him.

Eventually she found the toy she'd been looking for: the blue silicone vibrator that felt so comfortable against her delicate skin. Without packing away the other toys, she lay down on the sofa, her knees pulled up and wide apart. She lifted the minuscule tartan skirt Steve had told her to wear that evening and put the vibrator between her thighs. As the toy began to buzz against her swollen clit, she pictured Steve sitting next to her, stroking the insides of her thighs while she surrendered to the vibrations that were slowly turning the waxed triangle between her legs numb. In her mind's eye, he was running his fingernails from her knees down to the crease of her thighs, up and down, slowly and sensually, driving her mad with the insistence of his touch. She'd touched herself like that over the last few nights, hoping against hope that her attempts at his signature touch would make her feel less alone, but to no avail. The difference between his touch and hers was so vast as to be almost grotesque.

She reached down with her free hand, spread some of the wetness from her aching pussy to her clit and pressed the vibe over her little nub. As she rubbed the buzzing toy up and down, she imagined it was Steve's tongue flicking at her, licking her, driving her to the brink of insanity. The thought sent a pulse of pleasure coursing through her body that resonated deep in her pussy.

Within minutes she felt like her entire body was vibrating. Shuddering in delicious anticipation of what was about to come, she clenched her thighs around the vibrator as if it were a buoy that would lead her to the rolling waves while protecting her from them at the same time.

She was riding a small wave when the latch in the front door clicked. As the door fell shut, thudding in its frame, she realized with a start that Steve had arrived home, but that didn't stop her from pressing the vibrator against her clit as he put down his suitcase and leisurely wandered into the living room, shaking his head at the lewd image that greeted him. Nor did it stop her from pressing it even harder against herself as he sat down next to her, his jacket still on, his gray eyes full of mirth and terrible promises. Her heavy-lidded eyes met his as the tension she'd tried all week to ignore continued to build inside her, ineluctable and inexorable.

"Well," he said softly, arching a wicked eyebrow at her. "Looks like you weren't exaggerating the other day when you said you missed me, kitten." He reached out and found the moisture pooling between her thighs, eliciting a gasp from her. "I suppose I should consider myself flattered that my absence should drive you to this, but I'm a little disappointed that you couldn't hold out just a tiny bit longer." His fingertips began to explore her slick folds. "Would it have killed you to wait just five more minutes?"

Need pulsed through her body like a living vein, so hard that she could barely think straight. So intense was her need for release that she gave him the first answer that popped into her head. "Yes, Sir," she panted, her breath ragged and fast.

Steve seemed amused at her honesty. "I'll give you a choice, kitten," he said, sliding his fingers along her slippery labia. "If you stop now, and I mean *right now*, I'll forget that you went against my wishes, on account of your two-week ordeal"—he grinned—"and the fact that you make such a splendid sight humping that toy in that skirt." He traced the opening of her sex, teasing her beyond endurance. "If, on the other hand, you choose to go on, you'll pay the price for your disobedience. I'll grant you your orgasm. I'll even help you make it a good one. But there will be hell to pay afterward."

She glanced up at him with glazed-over eyes. "H-hell, Sir?" She could hear the breathlessness in her own voice, and the pulse that was thumping in her ears like the surge of waves.

He nodded, a smirk playing across his lips. "Thirty lashes with the rosewood paddle. On a wet bottom."

She gasped. The rosewood paddle was varnished, which meant that it left a mean sting. Thirty lashes with it on a dry bottom would be quite the punishment. Thirty lashes on a wet bottom would be positively criminal.

Steve wasn't done, though. "And no other orgasms for a week."

That was even worse. Worse and phenomenally cruel under the circumstances. Yet she knew without even having to think about it that she'd choose the immediate climax over the delayed ones. She needed the release. She needed it like she needed water and oxygen, and it was so tantalizingly, breathtakingly *close*.

"So," said Steve, his lips curving into a smile. "What's it going to be, kitten?"

She blurted out the answer without a moment's hesitation. "Now, please, Sir. Now." She moved the vibrator a fraction of an inch, trying to hang on to the maddening tension that was unfurling in her pelvis.

In answer, Steve rose to his feet, then sank to his knees at the end of the sofa. As his hands tilted her pelvis and drew her toward him, he looked at her from between her splayed thighs. "As you wish, my naughty, desperate, needy kitten."

A gasp burst from her lips as he pressed his face to her sex and laid a warm kiss on her entrance. She could feel his hot breath pouring over her pussy, making her lust surge.

Almost involuntarily, she lifted the vibe a little higher to give

Steve better access. The head of the toy hummed against her throbbing clit, sending endless ripples of shock through her. She closed her eyes and let the ripples wash over her, waiting for the big wave to crash over her and take her under.

As the tip of Steve's tongue darted out and rolled over her folds, from her sticky entrance to the smaller hole farther down and back again, Melanie clasped his head with her free hand, glad to have something to hold on to. She bucked her hips against his face and the buzzing toy. Flaring sensations were coursing through her body, building up to an inexorable climax. She knew she wouldn't be able to hang on much longer.

"Permission to come, Sir?"

Steve didn't answer. With a slow, measured thrust, he pushed his tongue deep inside her and drilled into her most sensitive spot, teasing her until her entire body was one huge, shuddering throb of need.

"Please, Sir?" she begged, her free hand trembling in his hair.

Again he ignored her plea. His tongue circled her entrance, making her writhe against him.

"*Please?*"

He briefly lifted his head. "Very well. Have your damned orgasm, wench." He bent over her again and speared his tongue into her, roughly and urgently.

Her head pulsed with a rush of blood. A tremor ran through her, racking her whole body with spasms of pleasure, and she squealed with rapture as the release she'd craved for so long ripped through her and set her free.

From beyond the bliss, she heard Steve murmur his appreciation. Then he withdrew from her again. As she switched off the vibe and rolled to her side, still shuddering with the intensity of her climax, she saw him walk to the toy box and begin to search through it. When he turned around again, his face still coated with her juices, he smiled his most devilish grin.

He was holding the rosewood paddle.

Melanie smiled back at him, a little nervous but not afraid.

The next half hour wouldn't be fun, she knew—or at least, it wouldn't be fun only. She'd be hurt, and chances were she'd feel that she'd made the wrong decision, that she should have chosen the long-term fun over the immediate release. But it didn't matter. All that mattered was that Steve was back and ready to inflict his cruel but exciting games on her again. That had to be worth a sore bottom. A sore bottom, and much more besides.

THE END OF SENSIBLE

Louise Blaydon

Tom was late.

A month ago—hell, *two weeks ago*—Jack probably wouldn't have worried about it the way he was worrying now. Now, though, the first thing that came to Jack's mind was the thought that Tom just didn't want to come after all, knowing what Jack was probably expecting. Maybe Tom was starting to regret this whole bloody thing. Maybe Tom had noticed that Jack was having trouble paying much attention to any lasses who weren't Tom, and maybe he was more concerned than Jack was about the fact that Tom had swiftly become his best girl.

It wouldn't be surprising, really. Tom always was the sensible one.

The doorbell buzzed. Tom was smiling, and Jack's first shameful urge was to smack him for making him worry, but then Tom really *would* be angry with him, and that was the last thing Jack wanted. So he swallowed the urge, though his "Took your time, didn't you?" didn't escape without a touch of cattiness.

Tom didn't seem to mind. Jack couldn't say he hadn't
noticed—the thing about Tom was, he always paid careful
notice to most everything Jack did—but he only rolled his eyes
and said, "Didn't set a time, did we? Anyway"—he started to
push past Jack into the vestibule, and Jack took a step back,
letting him—"I didn't really want to turn up when your mum
was still here, with these." He held up one hand, from which a
canvas bag dangled. Jack swallowed.

"I, uh," he said. His heart was thumping, but after his little
scare he felt the need for caution, just in case. "That for writing?
Or playing? New capos?" The band was the thing, after all. It
was 1963, and every poor bastard in the north was trying to
catch up to the Mersey Beat.

"Jack." Tom tipped his head to one side and smirked, and
Jack felt his pulse level out again, relief spreading through him
like oxygen. "Let's go up to your room."

At the top of the stairs, Tom disappeared into the bathroom
without a word, and Jack went quiescently into his bedroom
to wait. Probably it was stupid, this—waiting for Tom to come
out of the bathroom in his (god) girl's clothes, just so that Jack
could (*oh* god) take them off him again, but that was the point,
wasn't it? Maybe Tom shouldn't be the prettiest girl Jack had
ever seen, but there it was.

"You're miles away," Tom said. Jack blinked, eyes going
immediately to the door, and Tom smiled at him. "What were
you thinkin' about?"

He was wearing the skirt he'd worn the first time they did
this, with stockings underneath. His big soft eyes were kohl-
lined, something shimmery smeared on the lids, and his mouth
looked pinker than usual. His T-shirt, though, was just a black
T-shirt, and while Jack knew that girls did go around in T-
shirts, the fact of the matter was that this was the T-shirt Tom

had arrived in—maybe the T-shirt he'd been wearing all day, so the fabric would smell like him. There was nothing feminine about it. It showed off Tom's shoulders and the neat nip of his waist, his long pale arms. So really, it shouldn't be the T-shirt that was making Jack's fingers itch to take hold of Tom and pull him in; shouldn't be the goddamn ordinary T-shirt that made Jack ache to press his nose to Tom's chest and under his arms and breathe him in. It shouldn't, but Tom was wearing a skirt for him, and stockings, and *lipstick,* so it was okay. That was the understanding: as long as Jack was working his way into a pair of knickers, anything was okay.

"Jack," Tom pushed, mouth quirking up at one corner. "You all right?" He spread his arms a little, smile going bashful. "Is *this*?"

"Tommy," Jack said eventually, in a dark-brown voice, and he stood up, slid both arms around Tom's narrow waist. "You're a fucking cracker, you are."

Tom laughed and blushed, but Jack wasn't really paying attention. Up close like this, he *could* smell Tom, *real* Tom, cigarettes and aftershave and fresh sweat. His mouth went to Tom's throat, to the place behind his ear where it was all warm skin, and Tom groaned, head tipping back. Jack barely thought before he lifted him. He spun them, ignoring Tom's snort of protest, and tossed him onto the bed on his back. Years now, they'd spent sleeping in that bed after long nights of working together, singing under their breath when it was too late to make noise. And now Tom was on it on his back, legs fallen open and skirt ridden up, and Jack was going to have him.

He crawled onto the mattress, found the bottom of Tom's shirt and tugged it up. Tom laughed, sucking in his tummy like it tickled, and Jack couldn't help but notice the trail of hair that descended from his navel, guiding Jack down. Breathless,

Jack tugged the skirt down an inch and caught a moan at the blue silk beneath. They hadn't done this before, Jack realized slowly—hadn't been anywhere in the light where Jack could get Tom's shirt up, *see* him. It hadn't occurred to Tom to shave the hair off his abdomen, where a real girl would be smooth. Madly, Jack found himself hot with gratitude.

"Jackie," Tom said, half a warning, and then Jack's nose pressed into his navel and Tom shouted a laugh, breathless, muscles twitching against Jack's face. "Jack, don't!"

"Shut up," Jack told him, hot against his skin, and mouthed at Tom's navel, then lower, following the line. He caught the edge of blue silk in his teeth and tugged it down, half to show off but half just *because,* god. His heart was going like maracas; he got his hands up under Tom's skirt and cupped him firmly through his knickers. "Just let me, all right? Let me." Another kiss, low, and Tom's belly quivered. "Tom."

Tom let him. By the time they were done, they were naked but for the T-shirt and stockings Tom had retained by silent mutual agreement, though Jack's hands had mapped him everywhere. Tom was shaking, still, and Jack couldn't seem to stop rubbing his fingers over Tom where he'd opened so easy for Jack's dick, where he was wet. Against him like this, Tom could never have been taken for a girl. Not even with Jack's glasses sitting on the nightstand. But the stockings were still on, suspended from the little blue belt Tom had nicked from somewhere, so that was all right. It didn't make much sense, Jack had to admit, but they both seemed to be agreed on it, and that was usually the way bills were passed in the band. It was Jack's band, after all. It was all right.

That was the first time.

But it was like breaking a dam, setting a precedent that

couldn't be unwritten. So long as Jack could slide his hand up
Tom's thigh and find silk, nothing else mattered. Everything else
was okay, because that was what they'd decided, and that was
how it would be.

The first couple of weeks of it, they were, within certain
parameters, careful. Practice nights were for practice, and
nothing else. When they were playing actual gigs, it was worse.
There was something about standing on a rickety stage with
Tom, the glare of the spotlights making them sweat and Tom's
mouth almost brushing Jack's cheek over the mic, that led to
bad places. More than once, Jack had caught himself missing
his place in a song because his attention was fixed on Tom's
face, or the curve of his throat, or the line of his clavicle where
it emerged, sweat damp, from the neck of his shirt. More than
once, too, he'd stumbled off the stage breathless and half-hard,
voice scraped raw, and Tom had flashed him the eyes that said,
Make an excuse, quick. Then had come hasty bus-rides and
fumbled changes of clothes in Jack's little bedroom, Jack's hand
in Tom's mouth to stifle the noises as they rutted against each
other. But it was almost six miles back to Jack's from the George,
and the bus took its fucking time. And every set they did, the
urgency seemed to get worse. Jack found himself holding his
breath, waiting for something to snap.

The night something did, it was a Thursday. Not a hugely
busy night out in Newcastle, but a sort of amping up tended to
happen on Thursdays, everyone getting ready for the weekend,
desperate for Saturday to come. Onstage, Jack was feeling a
little desperate, too, hair sticking damply to his forehead and
smoke in his eyes. Tom was close enough that Jack could see
the thin line of spit connecting his tongue to his teeth when he
opened his mouth; could see it snapping when Tom grinned and

launched into the chorus. Jack wanted to be the one to snap that line of spit himself, tongue to Tom's tongue, tracing the shape of his teeth. There was one at the front that was slightly crooked; another a little farther back had a rough sort of chip in it, from where Tom had come off his bike and bashed his teeth on the handlebars. Jack knew these things, had felt them, learned them, like none of Tom's girls ever had. Tom caught his eye, and Jack felt a rush of possessiveness surge up in his chest like a serpent, violent and a little untrustworthy. God, but home was a long way off. Not for the first time, he almost wished he lived in a hut on the Quayside, just so he could get his hands on Tom that much quicker.

After the set, he gathered his things quickly. It had become a routine for both of them, however many irritated looks Keith threw their way, no matter what he muttered about the two of them being sissies all of a sudden, desperate to get home to bed. Jack slung his guitar up onto his shoulder and moved out into the dank corridor, waiting for Tom to catch up to him with a smile, and a "C'mon, if we run, we can make the bus."

When Tom emerged, what he said instead was, "Loos." He tossed his head, indicating, and at first, Jack didn't realize what was meant, what was up. Head still pounding with phantom bass and hours-ago beer, Jack followed him, but it wasn't until they got to the bathroom and Tom fisted a hand in Jack's shirt, tugging, that he realized.

He *realized*.

He should have protested, questioned, he knew that. But Tom was leaning his bass, heedless, against the bare wall beside the sinks, then reaching for Jack's guitar, and the look on his face was set, determined. Jack didn't want to interfere with that look. It set his heart fluttering in his chest, confused in a way that felt warm and restless and *good*, knowing that this was

Tom's idea; that Tom was taking responsibility for it so Jack didn't have to.

"Jack," Tom said, and his eyes flashed to the bathroom door before his hand moved from the front of Jack's shirt to his collar, then his hair, clenching in it where it was thick at the nape of his neck.

"The bus," Jack said, halfheartedly, and then cursed the impulse that had made him, but Tom was smiling, ignoring his babble, and the next thing Jack knew was the tension in his scalp as Tom's hand tightened, pulling him forward.

"They run all night," Tom said. He locked the door of the end stall behind them and looked at Jack, all wide dark eyes and mussed dark hair and dirty, unacceptable sex appeal. Jack wanted to pin him to the wall and rut against his thigh.

"Jack," Tom said again, low, drawing Jack's attention back, and then he was unzipping his leathers and Jack could feel his heart trying to fucking escape from his chest, practically; pounding and thundering like a washing machine trying to rattle out of its pins. At the back of Jack's mind, he still knew, still *understood*, that he shouldn't want this. Tom might have been a girly sort of boy, but he was still a boy, and right now, he looked like one, all sweat and stubble. But Jack was hard in his pants all the same, breath coming fast, and as Tom's zip went down, all Jack felt was his heart rate accelerating where there should have been disgust, should have been some sure, conservative, masculine part of him wondering what the hell Tom was doing.

Then he saw the flash of pink between the teeth of Tom's zip, and his heart stopped.

"Jesus Christ," Jack managed, voice a strained thread of a thing. "Did you—?"

"Too fucking far back home," Tom said, and shoved his

leathers down to his knees. Pants out of the way, that left only a pair of pink knickers struggling to contain Tom's dick, and Jack swallowed a lump in his throat.

As long as Jack was working his way into a pair of knickers, anything was okay.

"You sordid little tart, Tom," Jack said, voice breaking. Tom smiled at him, eyelashes dipped, and shifted his legs, spreading his thighs a little wider. Then Jack was on him, biting at his mouth, nothing delicate about it. There was no *time* for delicate in the sticky little toilets in the George, due to be locked up within the next fifteen minutes, but moreover, there was no time for faffing around when Jack had Tom there, pants around his knees and back against the door, waiting, ready. Ready for *anything.*

Tom was *loud.* God, they both were; that had always been the problem. Jack found that the moment he took his mouth off Tom's, he had to put a hand there instead, two fingers thrust between Tom's parted lips just to keep the noises in. By the time Jack had withdrawn those two fingers and worked them up between Tom's legs, Tom was shifting and squirming and moaning, and Jack stopped the sounds with his mouth, sucked them off Tom's tongue.

The toilet stall was too small for the two of them, really, barely big enough for one person, but they managed. Jack was too turned on *not* to manage, could have fucked Tom in a suitcase at the moment, probably, if it had been the only bloody option. He shoved at the tangle of Tom's trousers, dragged them down until Tom got the picture, kicked off one boot and tugged his socked foot out of the trouser-leg. That was enough, Jack decided, mind run ragged; the leathers were uncomfortable and clingy and he couldn't be fucking bothered to wait for Tom to get them off entirely. Tom seemed not to disagree. Jack maneu-

vred himself onto the closed lid of the toilet and pulled Tom into
his lap; shoved up into him and bit his lip as Tom let gravity
pull him fully down onto Jack's dick, head back and long throat
bared. It was awful, but the twisting heat in Jack's stomach told
him all the same that this was better—this, Tom in his sweaty T-
shirt and half-off leather trousers, face rough with a five o'clock
shadow—than any time he could remember with Tom in full
feminine ensemble, dress and stockings and makeup. This, *just
Tom,* was better, and Jack could stress about it; wanted to stress
about it; but Tom was in lingerie, still, after all, wasn't he? Tom
had been wearing those fucking pink knickers under his pants
for the whole set, and that thought set Jack's mind spiraling off
its fixings, Jesus *Christ.* Tom had played a whole fucking set in
pink knickers just so Jack would fuck him after, and Jack would
have had to be *dead* not to prickle with sweat at that realization,
breath catching.

"Jack," Tom rasped out, throat ragged and torn from hours
of singing, bitten fingernails pressed into the meat of Jack's
upper arms, "Jesus, oh, Jesus!" He spread his legs wider, bare
thighs sticking to the tacky leather of Jack's pants as he worked
himself up and down, back arched and tendons straining.

"Yeah, babe, there you are," Jack said, nonsensical, as he
fucked up into him, hair sticking to his forehead and self-
possession lost somewhere between the ache in his groin and
the look of abandonment on Tom's beautiful face. "So fucking
pretty, aren't you, aren't you, aren't you—*Tom*—"

The look on Tom's face when Jack emptied himself inside
of him was almost as gratifying as the look that followed
when Tom, too, spent himself, wet and sticky all over Jack's
stomach. Afterward, they cleaned up hastily, slipping out of the
back entrance since the front one had now been locked. They
shouldn't have done that, Jack thought, as they moved quietly

SLEEPLESS NEED

Monica Corwin

My hands itched, the blood hummed under my skin and I was starting to get the shakes. I grasped my coffee cup between my hands, the heat seeping through the ceramic, warming and steadying my fingers. It had been twelve hours and—I glanced down at my watch—thirty-seven minutes since I last had sex. The weight of him still felt imprinted on my body, even now, though his scent was long gone.

The diner I took up residence in was empty save the cook and one seedy-looking waitress behind the counter. I had ordered pancakes almost a half hour ago, and they still hadn't arrived. I supposed it was a good time to get some writing done. The pen that twined through my hair was blue. It slipped from its hold easily, the two other pens keeping the bulk of my hair confined to the messy bun. My notebook was already open on the table. I had just finished reading the last entry.

Writing and sex are my only two vices, each fueling the other and each keeping me at a modicum of control. I am a sex addict.

I want it all the time, no matter where, no matter with whom. Sometimes I can stanch the urge by reading old journal entries, but sometimes not. For some reason I was feeling it worse today than yesterday.

I tapped my pen down on the notebook, imagining last night's romp, letting it fill me up and take me back to his arms. The bell above the diner's door snapped me from the phantom lover's embrace, as did the beautiful specimen that entered.

Sharp and instant, the longing enveloped me. Each breath in and out of my lungs became more difficult as my body went molten. He looked around, his eyes meeting mine for a moment as he swept the room with his gaze.

I watched him as he sat toward the other end of the diner. His skin was toffee-colored. The need to run my fingers through the silky black curtain of his hair struck me, and I was on my feet before I could stop the impulse. The waitress was in the back somewhere, the cook nowhere in sight. I walked slowly across the black-and-white-checkered tiles until I stood next to his table.

One perfectly arched brow rose as he noticed me. I captured my bottom lip between my teeth, biting down, trying to take some of the edge off, maybe get out at least an explanation before I jumped him. We stared into each other's eyes, and I knew what he saw in me. A somewhat overly curvy girl with striking blue eyes and a smattering of freckles, with pens sticking out of her head. Not necessarily a wet dream come to life.

I cleared my throat.

"Hi," I started. It was not the most eloquent way to start what was soon to become an awkward conversation.

"Hi." A small grin played on the corner of his lip, and the only thing that I could think about at that moment was licking that tiny corner. I pushed the air from my lungs, depriving myself of oxygen so my body could get a grip.

I swallowed and gulped air before opening my mouth again.

"Do you think you could come outside with me for a second?"

His brow wrinkled but he must have been intrigued because he stood up and followed me out the door. The bell announced our exit.

"I want you." It was a simple enough explanation and oddly, it usually worked.

"You want me, like, you want to have sex? Right now?"

"Do you need me to spell it out with Hooked-on-Phonics for you?"

He chuckled, and even that sounded sexy falling from his lips. I was about five seconds from pushing him against the wall and enticing him to take me, but I was saved the indignity. He grasped my hand and led me to a pickup truck around the side of the diner. Even with the lust-filled fog clogging my brain, I registered the secluded spot and appreciated it.

He spun me around and lifted me up on the downed tail-gate of the truck. The water from this morning's rain soaked into my jeans but I didn't care. My hands were up his shirt, running across his already hard nipples. Like most Native American men, he was hairless, and it was sexy to feel smooth hot flesh under my fingers. The notion that I was going to take control of the situation was quickly divested as he shoved open my thighs and placed his narrow hips between them. His lips took mine possessively, and his hands tangled up in my messy bun. He was hard, hot and rough; perfectly suited to my current mood and the general cloudy gloom left in the air from the early morning storm. My senses woke slowly, reveling in the salty taste of his lips, the scent of ozone pressing around us. Most of all, I was attuned to the heat of his body soaking through my clothes.

I broke my lips away from his to focus on freeing the erection I felt through his jeans.

"Guess I didn't need to spell it out for you."

"You never did, I just couldn't believe my luck." The sexy smile was back but faltered the moment his dick sprang free into my palm. He was more thick than long, my fingers barely meeting as I gripped him. He growled when I ran my hands up and back down the smooth ridges of his length. That small innocuous sound sent a shock of longing through my body.

I was done playing games. I released him, took off my jacket, laid it flat in the truck bed, and climbed farther into the back. My jeans and panties came off before my ass met the jacket, already chilled from the wet steel underneath it.

It didn't take him long to catch on. He pulled his pants up enough to climb between my legs.

"Condom?"

My body was starting to take over, my mind blanking out at the onslaught of need coursing through my veins.

"Right pants pocket." My voice sounded hoarse and I no longer cared. The only thing that mattered was getting that penis inside me.

He glanced at my face as he slid the condom down, the end snapping in place as he checked the fit.

"Are you sure you're ready?"

I didn't answer, only pulled him down by his hips, fitting his head against my swollen, wet opening. He removed my hand from between us in an almost crushing grip. I started to shake as he pushed the end in only a tiny bit. Locking eyes with mine he delved his hand into my hair, releasing the heavy weight and scattering the pens with a plastic click.

The moment his grip tightened against my scalp he shoved himself inside me to the hilt. It was brutal and I cried out from the force of it, my ass sliding against my jacket.

I tried to sit up, to meet his hips with my own, but his hands in my hair yanked me back, baring my neck to his lips. He took full advantage, sliding in and out of me as he scraped his teeth down my neck. Some of the tension coiled through me released as my orgasm slowly climbed. He pumped in and out of me harder, using the end of the truck bed to gain leverage. My body was awake, alive, and I felt like Aphrodite herself being taken, consumed, utterly rendered by this sexy stranger.

I held on to his back with one hand, my nails digging into him. The other gripped his soft length of hair. Some of it escaped my hands and fanned out around us. A tendril here and there would brush my breasts, my waist, and it heightened my senses even more. My breathing came faster as I wrapped my legs around him, trying to crush his body harder into mine, my feet catching in the opening of his jeans around his knees. One of his hands was next to my head to hold him off my chest, the other was still tight in my hair, both of them closed in a tight grip. His hips pressed harder into me and my back bowed, trying to get him deeper, even though it wasn't possible.

"Fuck. I'm gonna come. Come with me, baby."

His words hit their mark, driving me straight over the edge. My orgasm crashed through me, wave after wave of poignant pleasure. Just as it started to wind down he slammed into me one final time, holding himself inside me. A grunt registered in my ears as he carefully released my hair. Half of his weight rested on my belly as he tried to regain his bearings.

The edge of the need was asleep, and now only the usual simmer kept me aware of my longings. I could deal with the simmer. I had done it for years. Lying still and languid, I waited for him to get off me, savoring the weight and heat of him, committing it to memory.

I would feel every second of this encounter later, once the endorphins left me and I started to feel the need again. I should have been ashamed. I didn't even know the name of the man still inside me.

He climbed down off the bed, baring my body to the chilly air. I followed him down and rearranged my clothes on before turning to face him. This was always the awkward part. To my surprise it wasn't this time. He leaned down and gently kissed my forehead, tucking my hair away from my cheek, then walked away.

I waited a moment before following him back into the diner. My pancakes were finally ready. I looked at him from my table, and he gave me a wink.

I smiled and started writing.

THE GIRL ON YOUR SKIN

Giselle Renarde

How could I complain? I was breaking my own rule.

Nesta and I made lots of rules when we opened up. She wrote them down in the back of her daybook, and we kept those pages pinned to the corkboard by her computer:

Don't bring dates home
Don't fall in love
Don't rave about how great the sex was
Don't come to bed smelling like another girl

The list went on, but I was hung up on that last point in particular. All night, I'd been tossing and turning in my sweat-soaked sheets. TV was boring. I went to bed with a book, but the book was boring, too. Brought out my vibe. Didn't do a damn thing. The room felt different when I was alone in it, when I knew Nesta was fucking someone else.

Waiting was killer. Lying alone in our bed, I waited to hear her key in the door, waited for the hinges to creak, for her to unzip those big boots and kick them off in the hallway. Even the sound of her breath, the shallow guilt as she tiptoed to the bathroom, flicked on the light, closed the door—it was all there, right in my ear. The squeal of the shower. I heard every step in the process like an echo as I waited for Nesta to come home.

I felt feverish, searching for a cool spot on my hot pillow. My head was burning up, and buzzing like a beehive. I bucked up against Nesta's side of the bed, smelling her hair, her perfume, her body. It was all there in the sheets.

Where the hell was she? Fuck, it was...*9:45?* How was it only 9:45? Felt like three in the morning. I covered my eyes and rolled onto my stomach, growling. My breath saturated the pillow, and I rolled again—onto Nesta's side of the bed this time. I wasn't going to preserve it anymore. When she got home, she was just going to have to deal with messy covers.

"Do you know what time it is?" I asked, in my mind. But that was a stupid question, because it wasn't really late. "I've been worried sick." Or maybe, "Who was she?" Or, "*How* was she?"

No, I couldn't ask that question. It was in the rule book. We weren't supposed to ask about sexual performance. I rolled back onto my side of the bed. More and more, I was starting to think it took a special type of person to survive an open relationship, and maybe I wasn't that special. Did everybody feel this jealous?

When I finally heard Nesta's key in the door, it came as a surprise. Maybe I'd given up hope or something, because I sat straight up in bed, on high alert, as if I thought the figure coming through the front door might not be Nesta at all.

She unzipped her boots, kicked them off in the hall. I couldn't see her until she tiptoed past the bedroom door, and even then she was only a shadow. The shower would come next....

No. Something inside of me was adamant about this. I whipped off the covers and stomped across the room in basketball shorts and a T-shirt. Nesta shrieked when I grabbed her wrist and pulled her out of the bathroom. She shrieked like she didn't know it was me, like I was some faceless attacker in the night.

I pulled her tight to my body and held her there, like we were dancing. Her breath hit my chin in hot little bursts as I pinned her against the bed.

"I haven't showered yet," she said in a whisper.

That day, for the first time, I didn't care. My lust for Nesta superseded any jealousy. I was so hot for her I didn't even know where to start.

Pressing her body tight to mine, I kissed her hard. She was too shocked to react, and I had to pry her teeth apart with my tongue, dig inside her perfect mouth.

Her perfect mouth tasted like pussy.

The sweet tang, the aftertaste that stuck at the back of my throat—it was pussy, unmistakable. And I shouldn't have been surprised, because I knew what she'd been up to, but knowing and tasting are different things entirely. That girl, that other girl, whoever she was, had found her way inside my mouth. She was a stranger to me, but her pussy was on my tongue. I could taste it.

"She fucked your face," I said, holding Nesta's head in my hands. My palms looked huge against the fine line of her jaw. "You ate her. You ate her good. Her pussy's all over your skin."

"Is it?" Nesta asked, like she wasn't sure if I was angry or what.

"Shh, shh, shh!" I didn't want her being scared. "Baby, it's all good. It's all good."

I licked her cheek and she shuddered. "Oh god."

"I can taste her pussy," I said, and kissed Nesta's chin with an open mouth. "I can taste her cunt. It's everywhere. That chick must have been riding your face hard."

"Yeah," Nesta admitted. "She was."

"Tell me what she looked like, girl."

Nesta inhaled sharply as I tore open her top. "Are you sure you want to know?" she asked. "I thought we said..."

"Forget the rule book." I leaned her down on the bed and kissed a sharp path from her neck to her nipples. They stood up hard against the cool night air, and I asked, "Did she do this, too?"

Petting my hair, Nesta said, "Yeah, babe. She did, but not like this. We were standing by the window, all the lights on. She stripped me bare so everyone could see, down on the street."

My pussy clamped tight when I pictured my Nesta naked, all eyes on her, getting her tits licked by some girl I didn't know.

"Was she wearing lip gloss?" I asked, because Nesta's nips had a tacky texture that didn't come from me. And they tasted like strawberries.

"Yeah," Nesta said. "Gloss over dark lipstick. Fake lashes. Golden eye shadow and thick black liner."

"A real femme, huh?"

"Yeah, babe." Nesta pushed down on her pants, and I helped her. God knows what happened to her panties. I'd never seen her go commando before. She must have lost them at this femme's place. Her pussy was bare where it mattered, with just a landing strip.

"You're still wet," I said, tracing my fingers over the slick line of her pussy lips. She was drenched with juice, just dripping with it. "Did this girl eat your pussy before you ate hers?"

Nesta nodded. "How'd you know she went first?"

I didn't know. I wasn't even thinking anymore. My body was taking her because that's what my body wanted. There were days when I wished to hell I could grow a cock and fuck her with it, fuck her hard. My system was in overload mode. Too much heat.

"Get me off," I said, begging for it. I didn't even know what I wanted her to do, exactly. "Get up on the bed. Spread your legs."

My cunt was throbbing for real, actually pounding like my clit had its own heartbeat. I pulled off my clothes as Nesta climbed fully onto the bed. Her top was open, hanging off her shoulders. Her bra was pulled down under her tits, but her bottom was bare. Even in the dark I could see her pink glistening. How much of that was pussy juice and how much was a stranger's saliva?

I'd never wanted to know before. I'd never wanted to think about who Nesta fucked outside our bedroom. But that's because I was scared. Scared these women were bigger than me, stronger than me, butcher than me, *better*.

That was it. That's what I'd been afraid of—that Nesta was looking to replace me, when all that time she'd been looking in the other direction.

I don't do feline and feminine. I like the look, but it isn't me. The girl who'd planted her face between my Nesta's legs had all that going for her. I could practically see her pouty purple lips parting to lap my Nesta's nectar. Pretty girls playing in front of open windows, for all the world to see.

My pussy pounced. Turning Nesta on her side, I spread her legs so I was straddling one, with the other launched over my shoulder. Yeah, I split her right in half and pushed my cunt right up close to hers. She shrieked and grabbed her tits, like that would protect her from me.

"You're crazy," she said, and I wasn't totally sure whether she was amused or afraid. "What's going on here?"

"I'm getting off on you," I said, pressing my fuzzy cunt right up against her. "Fuck, your pussy's wet, girl. You're all slippery wet."

I licked her smooth calf, and she moaned, thumbing both nipples. "God…"

She looked good like that, damn good, and I asked her, "Is that what you were doing while that other girl sucked your fat little clit? You twisted your tits just like that while she ate you?"

Nesta's eyes were closed, but she nodded. "Mmm-hmm."

"You keep tugging on those tits, baby." I rammed my cunt right up against hers, banging our bones together, searching for the sweet spot. It wasn't easy to find. Usually I'd have the patience for all sorts of bumping and grinding, writhing and adjusting, but not this time. "Squeeze your tits, girl, just like that."

Nesta pushed her big breasts together as I pulled her ass off the bedspread, holding her up until my muscles trembled. She wasn't heavy, but the effort got to me. I needed to come, and fast. I had to find that perfect place where I could rub my fat clit against her pink. I wasn't getting there fast enough, and it made me want to scream.

I pictured this girl, this stranger, between Nesta's thighs, lapping at her soft flesh. Would I be beat by some chick I didn't even know? Never. *Never.* I traced my clit up and across the plump folds of Nesta's pussy until I found what I'd been looking for.

An imagined tongue licked our clits as we grinded together—hot, wet, slick and powerful. Every woman had a tongue, but not every woman knew how to use it. Whoever Nesta spent the evening with knew just what to do. I could feel it like an echo in Nesta's pulsing body. I could feel it in the way she bucked against my pussy while we tribbed. There was something between us, something we could both feel even though it wasn't physically there.

"What's her name?" I grunted. I could barely speak.

"We said we wouldn't tell." Nesta pinched her tits and squealed. "It's in the rules."

"Fuck the rules." I pounded her pussy with my clit, making it a cock, fucking her like she wanted. "Tell me her name."

"Won't you be mad?"

Holding her hips aloft, I traced my clit over hers, feeling her shudder. I trembled so hard I couldn't speak. I didn't care about that girl's name anymore. I didn't care about anything. My orgasm was coming on strong, riding up my thighs and swelling in my belly before shooting straight to my clit.

It was fireworks, the way we exploded together. Her hips rattled in my hands. My cunt blazed against the soft, wet pink of her pussy. There was another element in the mix, too—a lingering scent, or feeling, or taste. Something foreign, not of us. Nothing else had ever felt this good, and I knew it was the unnamed femme, the ghost of a threesome. The tang of her pussy clung to my throat as I grunted Nesta's name. Her tongue was there on my woman's clit, lapping up hard while we climaxed together. The unnamed girl was there the whole time. No use denying it.

My arms lost their strength. I dropped Nesta's hips to the bed and our hot pussies tore apart, making a wet kissing sound. Falling in beside her, I spread my legs. My cunt felt so fat I couldn't close them without sending aftershocks through my whole body.

Nesta was panting wildly when I found her hand with mine. For a long time, we didn't say a word. We had way too much to talk about—a whole rule book to reevaluate. Hard to know where to start.

"I didn't take my shower," Nesta said, after a while.

"Yeah." I slid my arm under her shoulder and rolled in to sniff her neck. The whole room smelled like pussy, but I could still distinguish the one that wasn't ours. "You want to shower now?"

Nesta hesitated before saying, "Maybe in the morning. I'm too tired to stand."

We pulled up the covers and buried ourselves underneath. Change was coming, but the conversation could wait. We could sleep together in the scent of that nameless femme who'd taken Nesta up against a window, for all the world to see.

SPINNING

Kyoko Church

Don't move."

I don't. I try not to breathe. I hold stock-still. I worry that even my beating heart threatens him.

We lie there, a frozen tableau, like two people bracing for bad news, instead of like lovers.

I will it not to happen, not again.

"God, no, I'm sorry," Brian blurts out as he begins to thrust frantically.

Afterward I say all the things I'm supposed to say. All the platitudes. I don't know why I bother. He's not listening.

What I really want is to hold him. To continue touching. To kiss. Maybe even...to do something else? Satisfaction can be had through other means, after all. But he is closed up tight, like a clamshell. And right now, I'm staring at the white plain of his back.

* * *

The next day is when it all begins with WM.

I swear I wasn't looking for it. Not exactly. It starts inno-cently enough. I just sort of bump into him, you know how that can happen, and things just go from there. It's the old story. He's been in my life a long time, probably fifteen years. I just never looked at him that way before. When it starts becoming some-thing more than it has been, when it progresses to something physical I am surprised. Tentative. What will people think? We don't belong together. Well, not this way. It's so wrong. But as these things go, that is part of what makes it so right.

Maybe if things weren't the way they are with Brian it wouldn't have started. Maybe. But I feel such longing. Like a wilting flower desperate for water. Like bread going stale. So I do, I let myself. I let myself be with him. From the first touch, oh god, he feels so good. The thing is he starts off so slow. Gentle movements. Slow rocking. Lazy circles. He builds me up, over and over. Yes, he stops and starts, like with Brian. But all with intention. He takes me with such mastery. There is never any hesitation. He has a plan. From the beginning he knows how he will play me. He goes through each cycle of stoking my desire and he never wavers.

I can't believe how long he goes on. After all his gentle moves at the beginning at last he really gets going. He's rough with me. God, how I've wanted it rough! How I've wanted to be slowly stoked and toyed with and then taken hard! So hard. He shakes me to my core. "Oh my god, I'm coming!" I cry out in delirious bliss. I am, good god, I am. Not a whispering, simpering little come, trying to hold back, to bite my tongue, to still my quiv-ering insides. No. This is a shrieking, gushing, pulsing avalanche of an orgasm. I can barely hold on to him he's bucking so hard and so am I and I love it, all of it.

And still he doesn't stop! No, he slows down momentarily but then appears to switch gears and gets going again. "Oh, you're amazing," I cry, as a second orgasm is wrenched from my body.

I've read trashy romance novels where the heroine comes so many times she loses count. I hate trashy romance novels. I hate those silly heroines, ever beautiful yet feisty and plucky. I hate the stupid muscled Fabios on the covers, hate their long hair and hard pecs. But mostly I hate the writers for being so cavalier with their orgasms. Who has so many orgasms they lose count? I'd never heard anything so ridiculous! Repeated, countless orgasms only existed in the pages of those preposterous books. For me. Until WM.

I might reread some of those novels. Maybe they're not so bad.

Because I really do lose count. Five? Seven? All I know is I have never reached heights of ecstasy like this. I barely know what to do with myself. I can only hold on for dear life and pray that I will always, always have him to turn to.

"I've got a surprise for you."

A surprise? I don't want a surprise from Brian, considering the "surprise" I could reveal to him.

"Oh?" I say.

"You've seemed a little distant recently. A little...preoccupied."

I flush furiously thinking maybe he's seen something, sensed what's going on. But no, he continues, seemingly without pretense.

"Look, hon," he says, grabbing my wrists and pulling me to him. "I know things can be...a bit lacking at times. And that maybe I'm not"—he looks momentarily stricken and my heart suddenly goes out to him—"not the best provider." A strange way to put it, I think. "I want you to know, I can give you more. I can be the man you need me to be."

Guilt rises and swells and pushes tears to brim in my eyes. Oh, how could I have turned to WM? How humiliating. For him. For me. "It's okay, baby. It's okay." I put my arms around him, kiss him. He is the man I love, after all. For all his...shortcomings. As it were. I love him.

I press my body to his, embrace him expectantly. But he only gives me a little smile and a quick peck on the cheek.

"You'll see after tomorrow. I can't wait to give you your surprise."

After Brian has that talk with me I promise myself I'm going to quit this thing with WM. Just pretend it never happened. But now that I know what he can do, it's hard to control myself. Whenever I glance his way it's all I can do to stop from jumping him. I think Brian has to have noticed. The sidelong glances. The impassioned stares. Sometimes I feel bad for carrying on this way, right under his nose. But Brian would never suspect it. Not of us.

My pulse racing, my pussy throbbing, I wait till Brian leaves for work and then I go to WM. I have to. I am driven by an aching need that leaves me clenching and wet.

The words are always mine. He's the strong, silent type. But who needs words with his stamina? He can last an hour, sometimes longer, depending. Sometimes I want gentle. Delicate. He lets me dictate. I know how to push his buttons. He lets me tell him what I need. And then he delivers. He can always deliver.

I mount him. I'm on top, as usual. That's the way it works with us, but I don't mind. It's our thing. "Easy, baby, easy," I murmur as he pulses and thrusts between my legs. "Oh god, you're always so hard," I sigh.

After he's flung me around and my body is elastic with sated bliss, I go and collapse onto the bed, a worn-out smile on my face. Sleep envelops me. I don't even wake up when Brian brings the deliverymen in the house.

"Hello, sleepyhead," Brian says, a huge smile stretched across his face. "Have a good nap?"

"Very good," I blink back at him. "Wow, I was right out of it. When did you get home?"

"A while ago," he replies. "Your surprise has arrived."

"Oh?" I yawn, stretch.

"Come here and see it," he says, pulling my hand.

It takes me a second to realize what room he's pulling me into. When I see where we're headed my heart starts beating in my throat, a panic rises in my belly. He opens the door.

Horror.

A brand-new washing machine.

Brian beams at me. "I've seen how you've been staring at that old, beat-up one. I know, it was all off balance and shook all over the place. It was obvious what you thought of it. I could see you wished we could get a new one."

My mouth is dry. My stomach has bottomed out. I can't talk. All I can do is stare and stare at sleek white lines and shiny chrome.

"I got a raise, babe. No more making do for my girl. Only the very best. This baby is top of the line. Solid as a rock. I got the quietest, most stable machine on the market. You can hear a kitten purr over this thing. You could set your finest china on its lid during the height of the spin cycle and not worry a second."

He elbows me. "Ha, couldn't say that about the old clunker, could ya? So whaddaya think?"

I continue to stare in stunned silence.

"Aw, you're speechless. That's okay, babe. Hey, why don't we head upstairs? You know," he winks at me. "To celebrate. Although," he adds, loosening his tie and unbuttoning his shirt, "I have to warn you, I've been thinking about celebrating all afternoon." He blushes. "It might be quick."

SWEET REVENGE

Anika Ray

Buster's new girl's name was Janine. I found out about it because I called his office at the wrong time and got a message meant for someone else. Once I knew, it was so obvious that I wondered why I'd never seen it. I went in to fire her myself—if he didn't have the balls—and tell him we were done.

When I got there, I learned he'd taken her out to lunch. I sat at his desk, brooding on fire and brimstone. To think I'd once had dreams about doing filthy things on this desk. To think I'd told him that, and that my insides had quivered when he'd laughed! To think Janine—whoever she was—had gotten that fantasy meant for me.

I'd called him up beforehand, told him that the girl had to go or things would get ugly. At first he'd tried to give me attitude, but then like a punctured tire his voice went from angry to whining. I'd never seen him as less of a man. I said, go ahead and break it to her gently, asshole. I'm going to break you, nothing gentle about *that*.

I waited at his desk for him to return. Straighten things out.

I'd keep the apartment, of course. He could hole up with the hobos and the smack addicts, for all I gave a damn. I finally understood how Rhett Butler could have been such a fucker as far as Scarlett was concerned. Love had nothing to do with it.

I jumped at sound of the intercom.

"Yes," I said, voice like a snake going through the forest on its belly. Voice like a "Do Not Disturb" sign.

"There's a young man here interested in the now-open position," said Sally, all Midwestern sass. Now there's one he for sure hadn't fucked.

"Yeah?"

Probably some snot-nosed bastard. I wanted to eat this kid for breakfast, and I hadn't even met him yet.

"Should I send him in?"

I thought I'd give him the Eye of Death until he felt the Apocalypse coming. A good few minutes of the glare, and he'd run like the building was on fire. Then I'd feel better. I said, "It ain't my office."

Sally got a good down-home laugh out of that "ain't." She thought I was losing it. Well, what did she know? She'd never had it to lose.

A moment later the door to my chamber opened, and through the proverbial puff of smoke I saw the sweetest revenge I'd ever laid eyes on walk straight into my clutches.

I uncrossed my angry legs. I glared at the kid. Little asshole. He looked so surprised his big blue eyes bled sad eye juice all over the place.

"I think this is for the paralegal position," he said, as if his thoughts made a rat's ass hair of difference.

"Well, the boss is out right now," I said. Probably sticking it to Janine one last time, parting being such sweet sorrow and all that.

"Oh. Well, that's quite all right. I'm prepared to wait."

It wasn't until the leaf of paper cut through the haze that I saw what it was. He was handing me his resume. I looked at it, caught the "skills" section. Kid must have had every skill but people skills.

I said, "Sit down," and bit into the words like they were caramels. Like they were arteries.

"Thank you," he said, and then in a voice like a newborn lamb, "I'm glad to be able to interview with you."

Interview? With me?

And this is when the idea came to me, like that moment when they finally plug the damn Christmas tree into the wall and the whole fucking thing goes up in a wall of orange and green flame.

Fire in my eyes, I looked at him. Those baby blues, like I'd said, a narrow suit, a king's ransom of curly dark hair the likes of which I'd only ever seen on children. Any woman would have liked him, provided she liked them naïve, with big fuck-me eyes and a body like an ice-cream cone, made to be licked from the top down.

My tongue was itching to do that job. I looked at him again. He fidgeted and looked down at that junk resume.

I stood, and was light-headed in the sudden breeze that came off the recollection of my sins. My bare knees buckled only slightly. I leaned against the desk, and those electric-blue antennae on the surface of my skin were reaching out and brushing the black cilia on the arm of his suit, creating some serious friction. I crossed my legs at the ankle.

I said, voice like honey poured over a scarf of silk, voice like a lick of cool air on a hot day, voice like a tongue in the private forbidden zone of the Devil, "So you want to work for me?"

"Uh"—a moment of confusion, a fast recovery. "I thought

the listing was by a Mr. Martinez."

And here I scooched my little butt up on the desk a bit. I pretended to think about it. Then I shook my head.

"No, it was mine." Half mine, in the eyes of the law. Which meant half of this sweet morsel belonged to me too. I already knew which half I wanted.

"Oh." He was trying to look at his hands. I let him try. I let him fail. He had working hands, and I wondered where he got his calluses. Weight lifting? It could very well be. These Harvard boys were crazy about their bodies. Did I say Harvard? I meant, Hawford Community College. In Southern California. They called it the Harvard of Highway 63. Truckers' learning. The Ivy League of hard knocks. You get it. Life.

"You're going to have to demonstrate some of these skills to *me*, Mr. York," I said, and I suspended his resume like a condemned man, a foot above the bin. The wind in the room sighed. The resume went down into the bin on the errant thermal. "Now it's just you and me. The way I like it."

His eyes gaped like Bambi's, right before the forest fire, as I came over and sat down slowly, deliberately, in his gray pin-striped lap.

Let me tell you a little something about me so you can appreciate what that kid might be feeling. My soon-to-be ex-husband was once a Marine, then a small-scale politician. Neither career lasted long. The Marines discharged him for disorderly conduct, and he hired a spin man to cover it up just long enough that he could win election to city council. Then the whole sordid saga came out. His first wife, a TV anchor who realized she'd hitched her wagon to a star about to go nova, left him.

And that's how he met me, Wanda. Wiggling Wanda, Wet and Wild Wanda, Wonder Wanda. I had a three-part act at a joint right out of town. They said that when I was on stage, you could hear beer being poured ten miles away.

Buster came into the bar like Dick Hapless, fresh from his resignation hearings, the sad steam of failure rising off him like fog. In those days he still looked a little bit like a younger Clint Eastwood, rather than an older Dick Cheney.

By the end of Act One he'd given me a thousand dollars. By Act Two, he'd promised me a house on Cape Cod. After Act Three he came backstage and proposed.

What makes a girl say yes? The promise of immortal love? A brilliant wit? A nice ass? I wanted the house. I married Buster because after years of working the shittiest job I knew about, I was ready for the easy life. Now that wish had bitten me in the ass. Turns out there is no easy life.

But I still had what it took to make a sweet young thing like this forget his Mama, his school and the god he grew up fearing. I hoped.

I sat down and thought, it was now or never.

I wish I could describe what it felt like to kiss him, but it got lost in what came after. Yes, he was a bit rough around the edges, but nothing like the college boys when I was young. Compared to that, these girls nowadays got it lucky.

I eyed the desk, which in my mind wasn't just a workplace but a set. I got a wicked idea. I backed up, sat my ass down on that erection of polished wood, and winked.

"Let's do it here," I said.

"Do it here?" squeaked Hawford. His tie hung around his neck like a loose lasso. On that last word his voice rose like a nervous girl's. You would have thought it was the first time he'd done this. Hell, maybe it was.

"Oh yeah," I said, tapping the desk for emphasis. "Right here. Pretend it's the end of a long day, and I need you to help me...unwind."

"Yes, ma'am," he said. He went in like a diver, like a man prospecting for gold. I let my loose legs just open up and swallow his entire head. His tongue was like quicksilver, like a fish slithering in and out of a hidden cove. I pulled his head forward into my lap like I'd never done with Buster; I leaned back and let my hair dangle like a wild woman's.

"You ride that pussy, cowboy," I hollered, for emphasis, banging one heel against the desk. His face was glistening with tears when he came up. Like he'd had a revelation down there.

"Take your pants off," I whispered into his disbelieving face.

"Yes ma'am," he whispered, unable to speak fully. I watched as his hands struggled with the belt, the clasp, the zip.

"Forget it," I whispered, pulling him closer. I rolled up the edge of my skirt and let the pillar of his penis get at me.

We might have been a high-school couple kissing on the desk, but any close observer would have seen the join. I pulsed around him, hot with fiendish blood. His kisses were like little dots of fire on my face and neck. I held him close, kneading the tight dough of muscles of his ass, savoring the fullness, the power of it. I was the boss. My tissues breathed him in and out like water.

"Breathe with me," I whispered, letting our breath together set the rhythm for our movement. "That's right." The snake slithered in the garden; I shook like an arrow cocked in a bow.

"That's right, kid," I said. And with an internal boom like a cannon gone off, I came.

I slithered back against the desk. Watched as he picked up his pants. His bare ass was a work of art. I'd never wanted to see Italy, and now I'd never need to.

"I hope you'll consider my application," he said over his shoulder.

"Oh yes," I said, without even the barest flash of guilt. I watched him walk out the door, hips swinging. Sally watched him go too, then turned and raised her eyebrows at me. I shrugged.

It wasn't two minutes before Buster came in. The girl had been all over him. He'd been crying his eyes out too, I could tell. Like the comedy mask to his tragedy, I grinned from ear to ear.

"Kara—" he began, all the fight going out of him in a rush. For a powerful man, Buster sure didn't have much stamina.

"I forgive you," I said, all smiles. He stopped and sagged against the door frame like a man who'd been shot.

"Sure," I said, licking my lips and running my fingers over the whorls of polished wood carved into the edge of the desk. "We all get one mistake."

"It was a mistake," he said.

"It was," I agreed. He shook his head.

"You're too good to me," he whispered. "I don't deserve you. I never have."

I let him marinate a bit longer in his self-loathing and gratitude. Then I stood up and adjusted my skirt. Too late, I saw my panties were lying in the middle of the floor like a wilted flower.

"You know," I said, shifting my hips just enough to set his dreams on fire, "that when I came in here I was thinking naughty thoughts?"

"You were?" he said. God, men are too easy.

"Sure. You just get me all worked up." Hope dawned in his beady eyes.

"I don't deserve you," he said again.

And then, hammering the nail into the coffin: "You should hire a new secretary. But this time, hire a guy. A kid just dropped off his resume. Here it is. Must have fallen in the trash by mistake."

"Sure, sure," he said, his eyes still gleaming like polished beer bottles.

I hoisted the resume like a white flag.

"After all, if you hired a man, it would make me feel a bit more confident that you wouldn't be, you know, tempted."

she, bleary eyed and silently fuming until they reached their destination.

"We're here," he called as the car pulled into the drive. She murmured in sleepy confusion at being dragged from her gray and tired thoughts and looked out the window at the huge green mountains that surrounded them. The ancient set of wooden cabins before them formed the image of a resort with its own private hot spring, located deep in the countryside, hours away from civilization and the perfect place to reconnect. He got out and popped the trunk and grabbed their bags; she smiled hesitantly when he caught her eye. After all, it wasn't the first time they'd had to agree to disagree to make things work.

"That's a beautiful kimono," said the silver-haired innkeeper admiringly, stepping out from behind the counter to compare it with her own. The kindly old woman had snorted at the blush on the young couple's cheeks and leaned over conspiratorially. "They never do want to get dressed up, do they?" And she'd agreed and he had smiled and slowly they'd begun to thaw. It was meant to be a weekend to relax and enjoy each other's company, though now it seemed one to sort out their differences as well.

"Everything all right?" she asked as they came to the entrance of their private cabin. He paused, apparently wanting to say something, before he thought better of it and disappeared inside to toe off his sneakers. She made a beeline for the bathroom and had just gotten her hair down when he called her name. There, across from the battered old TV he patted the legless sofa against the back wall and handed her a dinner menu. The familiar way he asked, "Can you eat this?" at every turn, as though she'd never had raw fish in her life, was endearing enough to get her through, and with every tiny agreement they reached together the final vestiges of their fight disappeared into a soon-to-be forgotten past. The teamwork it required reminded them of why

they'd gone there in the first place; the naughty twinkle he'd
gotten in his eye as he finally eyed her kimono properly didn't
hurt either.

In the corner of the front hall sat their two suitcases, dropped
haphazardly; the main door was shut tight and a DO NOT
DISTURB notice had been added in case the hint was not taken.
Her *geta* and his shoes were lined up neatly along the highly
polished wood tile floor, but a trail of various cords, a wrinkled *obi*, *kimono* and finally some very Western, very expensive
undergarments were scattered across the floor from the hall to
the doorway of the *tatami*-floored room. A hastily cast off pair
of jeans, boxer-briefs and a sweater sat inside the door frame.
In the middle of the room lay a double-width futon, pillows on
the floor and assorted blankets crumpled at the bottom of the
bed—a bed which had formerly sat nicely against the opposite
wall overlooking a private terrace and garden. The reason for the
bed's movement was apparent: the young lovers had, in the haste
of their make-up sex, thoroughly fucked it across the room and
were now sprawled rather indelicately over its remains, sleeping
like two contented cats in the winter sunbeams.

The woman was the first to awaken, her bare breasts covered
in goose bumps as she rolled over to face her still sleeping
partner. He was completely nude and exposed and ever so quietly
snoring. The woman allowed her eyes to run over him then,
drinking in the sharp angles of his cheekbones, the narrow flute
of his lip, the long sharp drop from his strong chin to the deeply
muscled valleys of his collarbones. His chest rose in steady, even
breaths; the tawny brown of his nipples had been discolored
by her lipstick. She could follow the trail she had made quite
easily, the smudged lines of burgundy down his stomach and
over his hips and, rather tellingly, a perfect ring about the base

of his cock. The color and the feeling of drinking him in, of keeping him in rapture with only her mouth made the woman both proud and wet.

Watching him sleep, she began to grow bolder—not content with just watching any longer, she ever so gently ran her fingers over his member, which very pleasantly stirred and, much to her fascination and delight, grew thick and hard once again. *But still he kept sleeping!* She was amazed, baffled but tinged with the disappointment that he hadn't noticed; glad that she could still continue with her game.

Emboldened by her success, she leaned across him and lightly traced the seam of his cock, running her fingers from base to tip and back again, barely skimming the soft, delicate skin. She could feel herself becoming aroused again and allowed one of her hands to stray between her legs, caressing the skin that her lover had so recently lapped at hungrily. The memory of his ferocity overtook her; she could still feel the braided gilt ribbon of the *tatami* mats grinding against her hands and knees as he pounded into her, the slapping of his hips against her bottom, how tightly he had squeezed her breasts and the gentle sting of his teeth on her shoulder when he had finally emptied himself inside her. She hadn't come then. *He was quite selfish really*, she thought then, but now, this was all for her to enjoy.

She straddled his thighs then, (*still asleep and snoring, the nerve!*) and touched herself, pushing her fingers against her clit in deep, broad strokes until she was certain she could wait no longer. Biting back the moans that would have most certainly awoken her lover, she took that still hard cock in hand and slid it inside herself, the girth and heat causing her to pause, to enjoy the sensation of being filled under her own terms. Her lover seemed to have only faintly registered what had happened: he sighed and, ever so slightly, bucked his hips upward into her.

Throwing caution to the wind, she began to ride him, slowly at first, drawing him out and then deep within herself, then faster, pushing him inside until she could feel his balls bouncing back against her folds. She ran her hands over her breasts, playing with her own nipples with her head thrown back; she was undone, she came and cried out, her own juices rushing down between her thighs, running over his cock and spilling onto the futon. She stayed in place, panting, still staring at the ceiling when she felt two strong hands grip her hips and force her down farther than she had managed onto his now throbbing cock.

Maybe she hadn't been as sly as she thought: she had been caught and was now being punished for it. The hard deep thrusts were joined by something entirely unexpected: a thumb, apparently having learned something from her own actions, was working itself rhythmically against the almost too sensitive nub. He was merciless; she felt herself shaking as she sat pinioned on top of him. There was nowhere to go, nothing she could do but come, again and again as he punished her with maddening, deep thrusts and that thumb, forcing her to submit over and over. It finally ended when she felt him—felt it—spray inside her; the force of her lover's own orgasm making him animalistic, growls coming from the back of his throat through gritted teeth. Their cries must have echoed off the not too distant mountains because the silence afterward was almost unbearable. Her lover pulled her down against his chest and held her in place, his arms woven protectively around her as he cradled her against him.

"Better?" he asked, and then kissed her, a soft, reassuring kiss.

"Much," she replied.

"Forgive me?"

"Only if you do that again later."

THE BEAUTIFUL TRUTH

Sophia Valenti

'm sitting across from you at the restaurant, attempting to politely listen to your story—something about coworkers and lost files—but I'm failing completely. My ability to focus on what's proper disappears as I watch your lips move and begin to fantasize about them being put to a different use—one that will involve a slow, hot trip down my naked body.

You're wearing a suit and tie, and for once your hair is combed. It's sweet that you've tried so hard to make a good impression on our first date. I'll admit that I've tried, too. I didn't select this skimpy dress by accident. Scarlet looks good on me, and I'd suspected your eyes wouldn't be able to resist my exposed cleavage. I was right.

I smile and take a sip of wine, nodding in hastily manufactured empathy at your complaints about office life. I do care, but not so much at this moment. My main concern is getting through dinner and convincing you that I don't need dessert, even though you've never known me to turn it down in all the time we've been friends.

The rational part of me tells me I should savor this night. After many longing glances and much flirtatious banter, we've finally decided to do what our friends have said we should for years: date. You asked me out to dinner, not to "hang out" with you and your friends. You made it clear that your intention was a romantic evening for just you and me.

But I've waited too long for romance. It requires patience to play that game, and I'm all out. My desire for you is too overwhelming for me to endure that subtle dance.

You raise an eyebrow when I pass up the chocolate cake you know I love, but you're happy when I agree to your offer of a moonlit stroll. I suggest the long way to the waterfront because I know that commercial strip will be deserted this time of night. I have a plan, but in the end, I think it will suit you.

Outside, you hesitate only a second before taking my hand, but you quickly entwine your fingers with mine. And it feels right.

The barest hint of apprehension worries your brain; I know this from our talks. You're concerned that by taking this chance—by trying to build on what we have—we might harm a friendship we've grown to love and depend on. But you think it's worth the risk, and I *know* it is. We're great as friends, and tonight I plan to show you how well we fit as lovers. But I can't wait much longer for that.

Those thoughts are in the forefront of my mind as we head down the empty sidewalk. During the day, this area is teeming with traffic and pedestrians. However, at this time of night, the only sounds are the whoosh of occasional speeding cars, and they're few and far between.

Once we're a safe distance from the restaurant, my eyes begin to scour the storefronts. I see exactly what I'm looking for—a narrow alley between two brick warehouses—and my heart begins to pound.

"Come," I whisper, keeping my voice low, even though there's no one around to hear me but you.

You're confused—your mind set on that riverfront walk—but I toss my head to the left, toward the mouth of the alley, and tug your hand as I start in that direction.

My body is acting on autopilot. I've given up control of myself to my libido, letting it take over and steer us where we need to go.

In the shadows, I push you against the wall. I lean in for our first kiss—hot, hungry and laced with anticipation—and you join me in a perfect moment of unfettered lust. Years of longing swirl with our urgent desires, and I feel drunk with passion.

That kiss immediately unlocks something inside you, something primal and all male. Your tongue flicks against my lips, urging them to open. They do, and I let you in. You deepen our kiss, tangling your fingers in my hair as your tongue claims my mouth. I like that you've gone from polite and sweet to sexy and savage in no time flat. I always knew you had it in you.

I'm light-headed with lust, as if your kisses are stealing my very breath. I feel as though I might swoon, but you hold me tight and I manage to stay on my high-heeled feet.

In one smooth motion, you flip us around. My back is up against the bricks, their rough surface scraping my nearly bare shoulders. Your entire body is pressed against mine, and in this position I can feel the evidence of your arousal. Your cock, hard and insistent, presses against my belly; I feel it even through the layers of our clothes. Knowing that you're so hot for me, so fast, makes me ache even more for you.

Tugging my hair gently, you pull my head to the side and expose my neck. I allow my eyes to flutter closed as I concentrate on your tongue and how it feels skidding down my flesh. You kiss and nip at the skin above my collarbone, and I feel a jolt of arousal shoot straight to my clit. My lust now has a pulse of its own, beating wildly between my legs.

As my passion increases, I begin rhythmically thrusting my hips toward you. The motion does little to satisfy my demanding clit, but I know it's driving you closer to the edge because of the growl that escapes your lips. The sound unravels me; it's like I've never known the real you—the sexy you—but it's clear that I'm about to find out exactly who he is and what he can do to me.

That tantalizing thought is still swirling through my head as you turn me to face the wall. I brace my hands against the bricks—still warm from the day's intense heat—and my fingers aimlessly claw against the uneven surface as I thrust my ass toward you in a lewd offering.

You lean over me to whisper hotly in my ear. "It's been too long," you say, as you yank down my panties. Keeping my hands against the wall, I shimmy my hips to help you dispose of my undies, kicking them away when they reach my feet. "I want you—I need you. Now!" Your voice is filled with raw, unbridled emotion and makes me shiver. Goose bumps pebble my skin, despite the heat of the night.

The world outside of this dark, private space ceases to exist. All that's real is the rustle of fabric and the rasp of a zipper, and your hand at my hip with my dress balled up in your fist. Your cock is nestled between my thighs, barely kissing my clit, and I can't resist arching my back a little more, adding to the pressure that's making both of us crazy.

"Oh, girl, you don't know what you do to me." Your mouth is on my neck again, biting me so hard that I wonder if you're going to leave a mark—and don't really care if you do. Your harsh kisses leave me panting and gasping and breathing heavily between parted lips. You're rocking your hips, letting the length of you slide along my slit, the head of your cock gliding across my swollen clit and making my body quake. Before long, my thighs feel slick with the honey that's flowing out of me. I need you more now than I have ever needed anyone in my life.

"Show me," I manage to utter, my voice as ragged as my breath. "Show me how I make you feel."

As those words leave my lips, you plunge your cock inside me. A single hot, hard stroke, and you're balls-deep. My pussy's so wet and ready for you. One of your hands is working its way inside the bodice of my dress to cup my breast. As you pinch my nipple, I cry out loud and my voice echoes in this desolate space.

My fingers clutch at the wall, searching for purchase as I thrust my body back against you. You're pumping in and out of me, corkscrewing your hips to hit the most delicious spots inside me. We settle into a lustful rhythm, our complementary motions taking each other ever closer to the brink.

I work my body faster and faster. As your name falls from my lips, you slide your hand down my body, your palm settling on my mound. Your fingers ride along either side of your shaft, picking up some of my moisture each time you slide out of me. Using the evidence of my arousal, you bring those fingertips to my clit and press against it. One, two, three lovely circles and my body bucks wildly, my pussy pulsing around your cock. As my sex spasms around your shaft, you keep pumping into me and extend my pleasure. Holding me tightly, you thrust into me one final time, and I feel you throb inside me as you reach your peak.

After we pull apart, I turn to you. You're loving and gentle as you hold and kiss me, but the sweet, perfect ache resulting from our frenzied coupling tells me the beautiful truth: yes, we've been great friends, but we're even better as lovers.

WAITING

Erzabet Bishop

If you saw me on the street, you would pass me by. I am the woman next to you in the checkout line at the grocery store and two tables over as you eat dinner in your favorite restaurant. My build is average. My blonde hair is straight and long and I usually wear it in a simple bun or ponytail. Nothing fancy. My clothes are basic: blue jeans and a black blazer with a taupe blouse. Pretty conservative really. Until you look at my shoes and see the three-inch heels and a name brand that would take up more than a week's salary.

Hurrying down the sidewalk, I pause midstride to check my watch. Five minutes. My heart becomes a fluttering dove in my chest as I walk faster. Legs shaking, I balance on the edge of the curb, just moments from my destination. Every Tuesday and Thursday, for just an hour, I am alive. My panties are already moist and my hands shake, remembering the fullness of his cock inside me. Picturing the strike of a paddle across my ass as he lovingly stroked my clit into sublime abandon makes me weak with anticipation. Recalling our session last week charges my body with anticipation, and I struggle to walk faster. It is the waiting that makes me savor it all the more. I have to be with him.

The room is not far from my office. It is a private club in a nondescript building, one you wouldn't notice from the street. It too is hidden in plain sight. The room I am seeking is on the second floor. Sir does not like it when I am late. A pleasant flush creeps up my cheeks, and a secret smile turns up the corner of my lips. The thought occurs to me that maybe I should tarry a moment longer to see how much I can test his resolve today. Will he punish me? I shiver with anticipation, aching to feel the sting of a flogger against my flesh.

Entering the building, I nod toward the front desk. The concierge knows me and waves me on. The air is quiet. It is early yet, and most of the patrons will find their way here after dark. This is the way I like it.

Making my way to the elevator, I struggle to calm my breathing and my mind. My heels click on the marble floor as I make my way to room 304. The Black Room. I knock once and enter, eyes downcast. This suite is different from most of the others. It is a playroom with implements of my Sir's design. Here I can embrace the passion that burns my soul. My pale white flesh will be stretched out against the black leather of his world and I ache, waiting for his touch.

The room is simple. A four-poster bed surrounded with white sheers and sheets of the finest Egyptian cotton. A black-leather spanking bench resides at the end of the bed and a rack of implements is hung on the wall next to the door. It is a room of extremes. Pain and pleasure; both sides of the same coin. The toy box with secret surprises rests in the far corner. A dresser and a chair are near where I stand at the door. The wood on all the furniture is a dark cherry color, giving the room a masculine feel.

His presence overwhelms me as I see him standing against the bed, and I swallow. The anticipation of the last few days without him builds to a fever in my blood. I want to crawl across the floor and lay myself at his feet. Trembling, I steady my breathing and turn to him.

"Sir." I ease to my knees in submission, setting my purse on the floor beside me.

"You are late." His voice is velvet steel.

"Yes, Sir." I hear the brush of his slacks as he approaches. My heart leaps to my throat, and I have to rein in the desire that floods my body.

"Stand up, brat."

I rise, eyes lowered.

Sir's fingers stroke my cheek and trail down to tilt my chin upward. My eyes meet his in startled surprise. He draws me toward him and brushes his lips across mine. He tangles his fist in my hair and yanks my head back with enough force to bring tears to my eyes. His teeth nip at the base of my throat. He turns my head and buries his face in my hair.

"Undress for me, Linnet." The way he whispers my name in my ear makes my core quiver.

He steps back from me and watches me with hooded eyes darkened with desire.

My hands fumble with the buttons of my jeans, and I stumble as I start to kick off my heels.

"No. The blouse first." His eyes burn and hold me in place.

"Yes, Sir."

I shrug off the blazer and drape it over a chair to the left of me. I slowly unbutton the light blouse, letting my fingers linger deliberately on each button, and it slides down my arms in a flash of satin and lands on the chair.

"Now the bra." His voice is uncompromising, yet gentle.

I close my eyes and reach behind my back to unclasp it. The cups fall free and I let it drift onto the pile of clothes, forgotten. My nipples harden as the cool air from the room hits them. Shuddering, I remove my shoes, setting them next to the chair. Reaching for the zipper of my jeans, I meet his eyes for a moment and he nods. Sliding the zipper slowly, I ease out of the jeans, making sure I turn my ass toward him so he can see what I am unwrapping, just for him. Desire explodes behind his eyes like a chemical reaction. He moves backward toward the bed, eyes never leaving my body.

Naked except for a thin wisp of panties, I turn and face him.

"Panties, Linnet."

"Yes, Sir." I hook my thumbs in the delicate fabric and ease them down, tossing them with my other clothes.

"Present yourself. *Now*." His voice is gruff, and I can tell his lust for me has grown by the rasp of his voice.

My moist center has coated the inside of my thighs and I know he is aware of my arousal as I kneel. My knees are apart, shoulders back and breasts thrust forward. My eyes are lowered, but I can still see him stand. My essence is permeating the air.

"Why were you late?" His voice burns into me.

"There was a meeting, Sir."

"What kind of meeting?"

"It was of no consequence, Sir."

"Come here."

I rise and walk to where he is standing, next to the four-poster bed. It is large, with imposing wooden beams laden with rings perfect for being bound.

"Be on time." He moves behind me and I can feel the brush of his erection against my ass. He slaps me hard on the left cheek.

"That was for testing me."

I shiver in delight as his hands caress my breasts. Suddenly, he stops and grabs my wrists and holds them upward against the post at the foot of the bed. He binds me with red ribbon and brushes the back of my neck with his lips. My pussy begins to weep in earnest, longing for his touch.

I can hear him moving away and the snick of a drawer shutting. He has me tethered to the bed facing away from the toy chest, and I feel my pulse race with all of the possibilities. If I move my head, he will be angry, so I keep still, waiting.

"Close your eyes."

I feel something warm and soft brushing over my face and eyes.

"You will wear the blindfold today, Linnet."

"Yes, Sir." I squirm, waiting for what will come next.

"Brace your legs apart." His voice is firm. "Hold still. You will count for me. Each strike."

"Yes, Sir," I whisper.

The first crack of the paddle brings tears to my eyes.

"One..." I whimper.

"One, what?"

"One, Sir."

"Thank you, Linnet. Only five more."

The burn of the first strike flares across my asscheek and as the second one hits, I yelp.

"Two, Sir." My voice wobbles.

The third crack sets my teeth on edge and I let my head fall forward.

"Three, Sir."

He caresses my burning asscheeks, and I can hear him chuckling to himself.

"Oh my Linnet. Only three more."

He smacks me hard on each cheek, barely giving me time to count them out.

"Four, no five, Sir!" My head whips up, tears pricking the corners of my eyes, but I am surprised by the quick pops against my flesh.

The final strike stings like fire as he gives it all he has, and I let out a moan.

"Six, Sir..."

He gathers me into his arms and rips the blindfold from my eyes. Untying the ribbon binding me to the bed, he kneels down and kisses the tender redness of my ass, rubbing his hands along the warmed flesh. As he stands, I can feel his hard body press against me, and his arousal hard against my soft flesh.

Fuck me! Fuck me now!

"Come here, my dove." His arms surround me and draw me into his embrace. He is not done with me yet.

"I am sorry for being late, Sir." The warmth of him makes my pain recede, but the need to have him inside me is an inferno.

"Yes. I believe you are. Kneel."

I kneel in front of him as he unbuckles his belt and lets his pants slide down his hips. Removing his shoes, he divests himself of the rest of his clothes. His erection bobs in front of him and I feel my own juices begin to run sticky down my thighs, just looking at his large cock. He steps back in front of me and the musky smell of him invades my senses.

"May I, Sir?"

"You may."

I smile, and I crawl into place and take him in my mouth. The salty smoothness of him has me moaning, and I let my tongue wander around the familiar head of his cock and underneath, where it is the most sensitive. Sir sucks in his breath hard as I lick and suck along his thick shaft. His hands fist in my hair and I freeze in place as he begins to thrust his cock into my mouth. Opening wide and letting him in deeper and deeper had taken me months to master. He pulls hard on my hair, fisting it, and fucks my mouth hard. Desire pools in my center as he climaxes, and I taste the bitter tang of his cum as his cock spurts warm heat into my mouth and down my throat.

"Linnet." He whispers, smoothing my hair and helping me to my feet. "Come."

He sits me down on the bed. Placing himself between my legs, he pushes me back into a lying position with my feet hanging over the edge of the bed. He teases a finger into my moist folds and thrusts deeply. I arch my back as he eases yet another finger inside of me, thumbing my clit as he pummels my greedy pussy with his fingers.

"Are you ready?"

"Oh yes, please, Sir!"

Sir kisses me on the thigh and eases my legs wider apart. My ass stings from the paddle, but as always, the pain and pleasure only make me wetter. Sir eases my body over so I am facedown on the bed now, with my ass in the air. He stands behind me and his now erect cock trails between my asscheeks, and I feel my body quiver in anticipation.

"Open for me, Linnet." His finger again finds its way into my pussy and is coated with my own juices; he gingerly runs it along the satiny opening of my puckered star. I tilt my ass up toward him, spreading my legs, moaning as he inserts his finger just a little deeper and withdraws. He goes over to the table for a moment, and I can hear him playing in the toy box, getting ready to surprise me with a treat.

He returns, and I feel the brush of something small and cold.

"Are you ready, my dear?"

He squirts some lubricant against my tight rosette and works it in with his finger. Deeper and deeper he delves, widening me and making me moan with pent-up desire.

"Oh, yes Sir. *Please*, Sir." I breathe, opening my legs wider and willing myself to relax. My skin prickles with the heat of his touch.

Sir's fingers brush along my ass and then I feel the cold touch of my favorite silicone butt plug as he carefully inserts its lubricated shape into my rectum. It is small, but as it eases in and falls into place, my insides clench.

His cock brushes the entrance to my pussy, and he thrusts inside of me to the hilt. I moan at the feeling of fullness and close my eyes. He moves, the friction between him and the plug making my breath hitch in my throat.

He fucks me harder and harder. Smacking me on the sore part of my ass, he pulls out and brutally thrusts back into me.

I lose myself.

"Harder, Sir!" I scream. *"Fuck me!"*

"My, my, subbie." He growls in my ear and reaches beneath me to finger my clit. "Aren't we being a brat today."

He plays with my engorged nub and coaxes me into a screaming, panting fit. I am close.

"Do not come."

"Please, Sir. I can't hold it."

"No." He grabs me by the hips and plows into me with his cock, each thrust hitting the plug as my body begins to radiate with liquid fire, hurtling me to a point of no return.

"Come now!" His body tightens and I can feel the warmth of him as he erupts within me.

My orgasm comes in an explosion of fiery sensation leaving me a quivering mass beneath him. My pussy clenches around his cock, spasming with aftershocks.

Withdrawing carefully, his fingers trail down my body, lingering on my ass.

"You will leave this in until you get home tonight." He pulls me into his arms.

"Yes, Sir." I smile and let myself be tucked against him, replete.

"Ah, Linnet." His lips brush my brow and he eases me into a sitting position. Reaching into a bag on the table, he withdraws a box and presents it to me, wrapped with a red ribbon.

"My lovely sub. Will you do me the honor?" His eyes brimming with tears hold tenderness and passion.

I open the box and within it is a collar. Black leather tooled to resemble lace with silver fittings. Tears wink in the corners of my eyes, and I look up at him with love. He is the center of my world.

"Oh yes, Sir." Joy bubbles in my voice and no doubt shines from my eyes.

"Here. Let me." He takes it out of the box and fits it around my neck. His elegant fingers brush against my naked flesh.

"Thank you, Sir."

His eyes meet mine, all seriousness.

"Linnet. This is more than two hours a week. I want you to consider a full 24/7 lifestyle. Can you do that?"

"There is nothing to consider, Sir." I move from where I am sitting and lean into him, letting my bratty side out one more time before I cage it permanently. My collar burns bright against my flesh, as I brush his lips with mine and smile into his eyes.

"Master."

You might not notice me as I walk home, a secret smile on my face. If you did, you might wonder why a woman who was dressed so conservatively was wearing a leather collar in broad daylight. No one would suspect that the confident business-woman striding down the sidewalk is in fact a collared submissive. I blend in. Just like anyone else. The butt plug sends little shivers into my well-used pussy. Already I can feel the heat building up between my thighs. Sir is now my Master. My waiting is over.

LOVELY RITA

Harper Bliss

S weat trickled down my temples as I danced for the first time in months. I didn't care if Rita showed up. I boogied myself into a state of indifference I'd been craving for weeks. Pushing my arms above my head, I relished the predatory looks my exposed belly button received. Being declared too monogamous for Rita's standards didn't spoil me for this crowd. Just because I wasn't one for sharing loved ones, didn't mean I couldn't enjoy the thrill of a one-night stand.

A girl dressed in black leather pants and not much else swayed closer to me. I'd been working on my abs tirelessly since Rita left me, and now they were working for me. She pressed her hips into my behind and left them there, finding the rhythm with me. I guess you could call it dancing.

"Want a beer?" she yelled into my ear over the thundering bass.

I spun around to get a good look at her face. Hair tied back in a loose ponytail, some curls springing free. Intense black eyes and no makeup on her face. Zero resemblance to Rita.

"Yes, please." I shot her a smile. I was out of practice and fairly certain the sexy grin I was aiming for looked more like an insecure smirk, but she nodded and headed for the bar. I exhaled and brushed a strand of hair away from my forehead.

That's when I saw her.

A bundle of platinum-blonde hair. Lips red and full. A smile to die for. That glare that sent my heart racing and clit throbbing.

I gasped for air and scanned for emergency exits. Rita was not alone and I didn't feel like being introduced to her new girlfriend, who, no doubt, would still be so charmed by her she wouldn't mind all the talk of open relationships and the enrichment polyamory can be to one's life. I'm not one to judge—I just wanted Rita all to myself.

"I'm Liz." Leather pants girl handed me a cold bottle of beer. I wanted to rub it against my cheeks to make my burning blush disappear.

"Ali." I clinked the neck of my bottle against hers. "Thanks."

Liz followed my gaze, because, try as I might, I couldn't stop looking at Rita. She was the most beautiful woman I'd ever seen, with her big brown eyes and racially ambiguous skin.

"Do you know Rita?" Liz asked. I noticed the sudden twinkle in her eye, and I knew the score. This was a small-town club and Rita had probably taken half of the girls home at some point.

"She's my ex." It still stung when I said it. "It didn't work out."

I did try, but my heart had never hurt as much as when Rita had picked out a voluptuous redhead for us to have a threesome with. As if I wasn't enough.

"How long were you together?" Liz couldn't let the subject go. I totally understood.

"Seven months. Broke up three months ago." My night of

forgetting Rita was not going as planned. Not only was she here, but I was trapped in a conversation with a stranger about her. That was Rita. Ever present and always at the tip of everyone's tongue.

Liz whistled through her teeth. Any attraction I had felt toward her seeped out of me.

Through the crowd, Rita made her way to where I was standing, resulting in a crazy pitter-patter of my heart.

"I've been looking for you," she said, her voice breathy and low. "Where have you been hiding?" As if she didn't know.

The woman trailing behind her was so pretty it hurt. She had a relaxed hipster way about her. Maybe it allowed her to stand for things I couldn't possibly accept, no matter how much I wanted to keep Rita.

"I take it you've met Liz," I mumbled, avoiding Rita's question.

"Oh yeah. Good times." She poked her girlfriend in the ribs and flashed her a knowing smile. "Remember, honey?"

The gorgeous hipster was the honey now.

It wasn't so much anger rushing through me. After all, I could only blame myself for not being more compatible with Rita's ways. It was a big surge of raw lust gripping me at the sight of Rita's neck and her skin the color of brown butter. I had always wanted Rita. From the first second I laid eyes on her until this moment in the club, downgraded to the word *ex*, huddled between her current girlfriend and a lover for one night.

It was madness, still my blood pulsed with desire. Hot pangs of want were speeding through my veins. Heat gathering between my legs already. One look was always all it took.

"Please, meet Anya." When Rita smiled at Anya it was as if someone reached into my chest and squeezed a cold fist around my heart. I'd never get that smile again. I'd relinquished all rights to it the day I disagreed with Rita's rules.

"Hey." Anya waved a long-fingered hand at me. She was a skinny jeans and tank top kind of woman, with long ash-blonde hair falling to her shoulders and subtly painted lips.

"Let's dance." Rita grabbed Anya's hand and pulled her onto the dance floor. Then she had the audacity to wink at me. My breath hitched in my throat and all I wanted was to drag her away from Anya and take her home. Have her do that thing she did to me. That thing no one else ever did.

Liz and I followed. She seemed as entranced as I was, the twinkle in her eye still present. We slithered our bodies between sweaty arms and backs and I started moving with the rest of them. Whenever I glanced in Rita's direction, which was about 95 percent of the time, her eyes were fixed on me. I knew that look. She knew I did.

No one danced like Rita. The music flowed through her bones and her muscles flexed and relaxed to the beat of its drum. It inhabited her and she was all the more mesmerizing for it. Plus, she kept eyeing me.

I finished the beer Liz bought me in a few long drags and made for the bar to replenish, needing a break from Rita's stare. It was obvious what she was playing at.

Drops of sweat flickered on her bare shoulders when she joined me at the bar. I ordered four beers and thrust one in her hand.

"Thanks," she said, while letting her finger glide over the back of my hand. "I'm so thirsty." She tilted her head back, exposing the delicate skin of her neck, and swallowed for what seemed like an eternity. "Anya likes you."

In a perfect world, I would have been over Rita by then. I tried to look away and ignore her, but the muscles in my neck didn't allow me to—as if they were still as infatuated with her as the rest of me. Instead, I stared into the brown of her eyes, took in the enormity of her smile and surrendered. I'd never be done with her.

"Do you want to play?" She inched closer. So close I could feel her breath on my cheeks. "Liz is welcome to join as well, of course. She's fun."

It was her unwavering confidence that always got me. Not a lot of people said no to her, because she acted as if it wasn't even a possibility.

She brought her lips to my ear. "I know what you like."

I could barely move. She'd whispered me straight into a frenzy of desire. I inhaled and exhaled slowly to regain composure.

"I'd better get these to the others." I pointed at the bottles of beer on the counter.

She slanted toward me again. "I'll take that as a yes."

She wasn't too far off.

I weighed my options as if I had any. As if Rita's proposal hadn't erased all other outcomes to my night.

I could go home alone. I could take Liz home. All four of us could go somewhere together. Or I could ditch Liz—one less contender for Rita's attention. None of the possibilities had me alone in a room with Rita, but beggars can't be choosers.

My hands trembled when I brought the bottle to my mouth. My body wasn't giving me a lot of options. Throughout the seven months of our affair it had been reduced to nothing more than a bundle of want. Attraction-wise, no one came close. If she was offering it on a silver platter, I wouldn't say no—even if it meant including Anya. Even if it meant I was the extra for the night.

I found Rita's eyes, bit my lip and nodded. The smile she shot me alone was enough to send me reeling. She arched her eyebrows and tilted her head in Liz's direction, silently questioning her inclusion. I shook my head. If I was sharing Rita, one other person would do.

Fifteen minutes later, Rita, Anya and I sat huddled together in the backseat of a cab. I felt my blood beat through my veins as Rita's thigh flanked mine. It was only fitting she resided in the middle, like a queen amidst her minions. I wondered if Anya was as much a sucker for Rita's touch as I was. The answer was obvious.

Rita's flat hadn't changed. It was all red mood lighting and shag carpet. A faux fireplace guarded by life-size leopard statues in black marble. In anyone else's home it would have looked tacky.

"Hey." Rita pounced on me like a wildcat while Anya watched. Was she more of an onlooker? I hoped she was.

Rita's blood-red lips came for me. Her heady perfume hit my nostrils hard, and I inhaled as if my life depended on it. Her nipples poked into my skin through the fabric of our tops, and the prominent display of her arousal flattered me.

"You're in for a treat." There was that unflinching confidence again. There was no doubt in my mind that she was right. Every second with Rita was a treat.

Her fingers dug into my scalp as she kissed me, and my legs turned to jelly. Her smile shifted from generously broad to mischievously narrow as she pulled her mouth away from mine and glanced at me. She all but licked her lips.

"Come on." She grabbed my hand and guided me to the bedroom. I had fond memories of Rita's king-size bed, which, from my point of view, was a total waste of space because I always slept glued to her caramel-skinned body. She probably bought it with more advanced sexual activities in mind. It could easily fit three.

Anya followed us and hoisted her top over her head as

soon as we entered the bedroom. All my attention had been
so focused on Rita, I hadn't even noticed she'd gone through
the night braless. As if it was a practiced routine, Anya inched
closer and Rita stepped back.

"Kiss for me." Rita sat down on the bed, sucking her bottom
lip between her teeth.

Anya's nails scraped over the flesh of my arms. A crooked,
full-lipped smile played around her lips. She looked so pale
compared to Rita.

She pressed her naked chest into me, rigid nipples stabbing
into my breasts, and traced the tip of her tongue along my neck,
over my chin, to my mouth. The room was silent except for the
agitated coming and going of our breath and the touching of
our lips. Rita sat stock-still on the edge of the bed, her eyes on
fire and her head tilted sideways.

Despite it not being Rita on the receiving end of my kisses,
the fact that she sat watching us was enough of a turn-on. Anya
tugged at my T-shirt and I lifted my arms to allow her to take it
off. After she one-handedly unclipped my bra, she leaned into
me and breathed heavily into my ear.

"We're going to make you come so hard," she said, and it
made me shiver. That was Rita's line. That's how I knew she
spoke the truth.

My nipples stiffened into hard peaks as they grazed Anya's
porcelain skin. She slid a finger under the waistband of my
jeans and flipped the button open. Before coaxing me toward
the bed, she lowered the zipper with her other hand, and pushed
me down.

I found her eyes and saw the madness, the same madness
I'd seen flicker in Rita's gaze so many times. The yearning for
this kind of activity. The desire to live with an abandon foreign
to me.

From the bottom of the bed, Rita yanked at my jeans until they slid off. Anya removed her own trousers faster than I could blink. She didn't appear to wear any panties either. It figured.

Anya lay down next to me and, while circling one finger around my belly button, allowed me to enjoy the show of Rita undressing herself. The spectacle wasn't in the way she did it, slowly and totally aware of the effect she had on me, but more in how she held my gaze throughout it. The intensity brimming in her eyes left me panting underneath Anya's tickles. Her glance skimming over my bare skin was plenty of incentive for my clit to swell beneath the flimsy fabric of my panties.

As soon as Rita was undressed she hopped on the bed and pressed her body against my side.

"Let me prove to you once and for all"—Rita looked me square in the face—"that three pairs of hands are so much better than two."

Anya's circling motions traveled up to my chest, while Rita started stroking my inner thighs. She might have had a point.

Their lips found each other over my head and, instead of jealousy, bursts of sweltering lust rushed through me.

Anya, on my left, pinched my nipple hard as Rita, on my right, trailed the top of her finger over the crotch of my panties. They broke their lip-lock to bestow all of their attention on me, and yes, it felt as if I were being fondled by a million hands at the same time. Fingers were everywhere. A frenzy of pecks, lingering tongues and thrilling pinches descended on me.

Rita dragged my panties off me and my swollen pussy lips pulsed for her. Anya let a fingertip skate over my hard nipples while driving her tongue deep into my mouth. Instinctively, I spread my legs for Rita. I was so hot for her, so ready. The club, the cab ride, the little show—rehearsed lines and all—they had put on for me, it was all foreplay and I didn't need any more gentle coaxing. Juices oozed out of me as my clit throbbed to the quickening beat of my heart.

Anya moved the action of her mouth to my breasts and sucked a nipple between her lips. Rita trailed a finger through my wetness and I shivered in my skin. My muscles trembled and I pushed myself up to meet her, eager for her to enter. Her lips parted slightly as she slipped a finger inside.

"Oh god," I moaned, because Rita's finger inside of me was all I ever wanted. She soon added a second one, while Anya nibbled on my nipples, her hands kneading and her teeth grazing.

With her free hand, Rita pulled the skin away from my clit, exposing it to the musky bedroom air. She didn't touch it; she just watched it as my juices gathered in the palm of her hand.

"Ready?" she asked, a surprisingly solemn expression on her face.

"Oh," I hissed in reply, no longer able to form words. I knew what she meant though, and my skin flared with anticipation. I was lost beneath their hands and tongues. A willing victim of their double act.

Rita curled her fingers inside of me and found the spot. The one, somehow, only she could reach. In response, I arched my back, my muscles stiffening. Anya's hand and lips kept arousing me, propelling me to new heights. Rita's fingers pushed inside, circling, curling, bringing me to the brink.

I found Rita's eyes and drank in her desire, because in that moment, she was mine. Or I was hers—again. All signs of irony had left her face. She pinned her gaze on me while her fingers touched me inside, the intent of them displayed in the twitch of her lips. Witnessing how Rita wanted me was all I ever needed. It wasn't a magical spot inside of me yearning to be stroked; it was the passion in her eyes and how it connected with every fiber of my being.

It started in my belly, a wildfire spreading through my flesh, seizing me. My pussy tingled and my nipples reached up. Flames tickled my skin. Desire burned through my bones.

I cried out as I came, fingers on my nipples and in my cunt. The climax echoed through me, bouncing through my body, again and again. I clenched the walls of my pussy around Rita's fingers, as though I never wanted to let her go again, before collapsing into the mattress, spent and voiceless.

Rita gently slid out her fingers, dragging them along my belly, coating my skin in my own wetness, and kissed me on the mouth.

"I told you," she said.

Anya kissed my left cheek and Rita pressed her lips against my right cheekbone.

I curved my arms around the pair of them before turning my face to Rita. "Lesson learned."

BLUE BALLS

Kissa Starling

A shrill ring trilled when he walked through the door. No light showed past the heavy tapestries hanging from the walls. Knickknacks littered the shelves. A fountain, directly in front of the door, cycled water around. Sandalwood incense rose to form layers of smoke. Gus took short, hesitant steps into the store.

Thick carpet muffled the storekeeper's approach.

For the tenth time since walking across the parking lot he wondered about taking advice from his friend Gary. He'd almost decided to leave when a voice boomed in his direction.

"May I help you?" The massive-bosomed woman leaned close, draping a purple scarf across her face. "Are you here for a reading perhaps?" Red paint covered her bulbous lips. Her long nails scraped along his forearm. "Looking for love or money?"

Gus backed away, stammering. "I'm not sure."

"Of course you're not. You're tired of the time dating takes away from your work. And you despise women who sleep over.

You don't like to share your money...with anyone." She produced a fan from beneath her girth, moving it back and forth in front of her sweaty face.

"Actually, that is true. I'm focusing on my career right now. There are things I want in life and women don't factor into that." He couldn't believe he'd said it out loud. His Jewish mother would gasp.

"So what's the problem, dearie? Work twenty-four hours a day and make tons of money. Happy Gus, right?" Her fan disappeared. Gus noticed a sort of jeweled bracelet attached to her foot when she hefted her body behind the counter.

He puffed up, puzzled. "How do you know my name?"

"Does it really matter?" It was a rhetorical question he guessed, since she bent down to search for something, ignoring his words. "I have what you want. Just have to find it." Several items fell to the floor during her search. She moved boxes and broke a glass owl.

"This is a mistake. Thanks anyway." Gus hurried to the exit. He pushed the swinging door open....

"Found it."

Gus shut his eyes, dueling with his conscience. *This lady is crazy, but it will only take a minute to see what she's got. I can't imagine it being something I want.* Decision made, he turned, letting the door shut on itself.

The gypsy woman held something in her hand. Gus squinted, sizing up the small box she held in her open palm. "As I said, nothing you need or should even have, but I believe you want it. All the workaholics want it."

She dumped it into his hand when he reached the counter. The wooden box had symbols scratched into it. "Do you know what these mean?"

"I don't. That box was here when I bought the place." She

rapped fingernails on the glass next to the register. Without asking if he wanted it, she rang the purchase up. "Three hundred dollars." Her empty palm waited.

"For this?" Gus contemplated handing the box back, but changed his mind at the last second. "Here." He handed her his credit card. Three minutes later he was the proud owner of a wooden box that he hadn't even opened. He rushed for the door and this time had no difficulty exiting the establishment.

Fresh air replaced stale air in the parking lot. Gus took a deep breath and then jumped into his car, starting it and peeling away on the road toward home without fastening his seat belt. He flung the small wooden box onto the passenger seat. One mile later, at a red light, he retrieved the box and opened it. A set of blue balls, connected in the middle, had a number etched on the wooden handle: 100.

Gus opened the box to throw the strange item back in, touching opposite ends as he did. Two things happened: His dick hardened, and it began pulsating on its own. He gripped the steering wheel, smiling at the lady in the car next to him. His whole body tightened and cum soaked through his pant leg and onto his car seat.

"What the hell was that?" Gus picked the blue balls up with his thumb and forefinger, dropping them back in the box. The number now read 99.

"Damn. That may be the best three hundred dollars I've ever spent. I didn't have to take time for dinner, idle chat or flirting." Gus closed the box and stuffed it into his glove box right when the light turned green. That night he dreamed of naked ladies in every shape and size. Some were light skinned and others were dark, but they were all nude and holding their arms out to him. Funny, since he didn't need women at all anymore. No more spending money on dinner just to be disappointed. No more casual conversations over topics he cared nothing about. He had a sure thing, halleluiah.

The next morning Gus woke with a smile. He dressed, dashed to work and entered the office before anyone else. His computer powered up while he poured his own coffee. Stock tips were soon displayed in multiple windows on his PC.

"Good morning, Mr. Rickman." His secretary, Suzie, stood by her desk, with her huge smile and dimples, same as every other morning. Her disposition irked him.

Gus didn't acknowledge her greeting but ran past her yelling, "Hold the elevator." Steel doors opened to dump out commuters and he slipped inside. When the elevator reached the parking level, Gus was the first one out, and he sprinted back to his car. Two clicks, a beep and his door unlocked.

He removed the wooden box and tucked it into his jacket pocket. Since everyone else had taken an earlier elevator up, he made this trip alone. His gaze wandered back and forth; he covered the camera with his jacket. The box flipped open and he held the blue balls in his hand, opposite ends simultaneously. A tingling began at his feet and traveled through his body. Gus jumped to take the handkerchief from his suit pocket, and unzipped his trousers. He squeezed his buttocks together. The energy surged to his dick and exploded. Cum squirted into the ready cloth. "Ahhh, I needed that." Gus zipped his pants and tucked his shirt back in before the doors opened. He even remembered to take his jacket down and slip it on while making his way back to his office.

"Do you need anything, Mr. Rickman?" There she was again, always so damn nice.

"No, Suzie, I don't." He dropped the soiled cloth into the wastebasket on the way past.

Gus made two high-profile deals, no problem, but it took

him an hour. He glanced at his watch repeatedly. "I'm taking an early lunch, Suzie. I'll be back by two o'clock."

"But, sir. It's only nine in the morning. I have these folders for you to look over." She stood there, waiting, as if she had power over him. No woman had power over him.

"It's a working lunch. Set the folders on my desk."

"Would you like for me to hold that box at my desk while you're gone?" Her cheery simpleton eyes gazed at him from behind rhinestone glasses.

"No!" he shouted, not bothering to apologize on the way out. She gasped, holding her hand to her throat in shock.

Gus stopped for a short time in the men's restroom to touch the balls and stock up on paper towels. That was the first time he came from anal stimulation. Those balls knew no bounds where kink was concerned. He flipped his arm over ten times looking at his watch in the elevator. Only one orgasm proved to be possible in the parking deck because the part-timers were commuting in. The number changed to 93 as he slid into the driver's seat. Nine miles to his apartment building and he drove like a crazed person the whole way. Every time he attempted to take out the blue balls a policeman pulled up behind or beside his car. *Damn.*

He ran up the stairs to his apartment, flinging the door open and fumbling with the wooden box because his hands were shaking. *86.*

Twelve orgasms later, Gus collapsed on his couch, naked. *Life is good.* He fell asleep. Women with three tits and two pussies invaded his dreams. He shunned all of them. "I don't need you," he shouted. "I have blue balls." One sweet girl-next-door approached him, but he flipped her the bird. "I have what I want."

Sun streamed through the patio door. He'd forgotten to shut

the drapes. That meant his neighbors could see inside, but Gus didn't care. He reached for the balls; always back in the box when he needed them. His nipples poked out while his dick lengthened. "Yeah, baby. Give it to me." He paused for half a second. *Did I just talk dirty to an inanimate object?* A hard grasp took his dick, milking it. *Oh, so warm and nice.* Cum spread across his belly. *64.*

Gus turned the television on right before the phone rang.

"Mr. Rickman?" That sweet sickening voice again.

"Yes, Suzie. What is it? I'm busy." Gus reached for the blue balls while still on the phone.

"Well, sir. You never came back after your long lunch and I just wondered if you're planning on coming in today?" She hesitated after enunciating *today* with the tip of her tongue. He could hear the snobby tone of her voice. How annoying.

"I'm sick, Suzie. Have you ever known me to miss a day of work?" His voice got gruff as his dick rubbed against the rough fabric of the sofa. He threw in a few loud coughs.

"No. Of course not, sir. I do hope you feel better. Should I bring you soup or tissues?"

Gus screamed into the phone, "No," and hung up. That orgasm brought him down to *47.*

Three days later, hungry and dehydrated, Gus ordered pizza. He happened to be in the middle of an orgasm when the deliveryman got there.

Knock, knock.

"Hello, is anyone home?"

The pimply teen took the pie and walked back to his car before Gus could get to the door, another opportunity missed.

Lack of food had drained him. He attempted to crawl to the door, but didn't make it before the driver was gone. Gus looked at the broken phone. He'd thrown it across the room the last time Suzie called. The mirror it hit lay on the floor in front of him. Luckily it hadn't broken. He didn't need seven years of bad luck. In it he saw a reflection of the blue balls, which lay in the box on the end table. *11.*

A week later he dared to look into the mirror. An old man looked back at him. Stubble had grown into a short, scraggly beard. Red eyes drooped from lack of sleep. His teeth had yellow goo on them. Gus disgusted himself. The dropping number scared him. *How will I have sex without it?*

Gus ate cold soup from a can to replenish his energy. He drank sour milk, spitting it up and remembering he hadn't shopped in days. Dressing was a cumbersome chore. He refused to put the blue balls down. They felt comfortable in the palm of his right hand. It took everything he had left in him to make it to the car, but he did and he drove straight to the gypsy's shop without stopping. *1.*

The most extreme orgasm he'd ever experienced hit while he was walking through the door, as the bell rang. He clung to the door frame, convulsing with pleasure. He hadn't meant to touch them. Smooth wood replaced the number etching and the blue balls were now a pinkish color.

Behind the counter the gypsy stood fiddling with her merchandise. He collapsed, chest on the counter. "Fix it. You have to make it work." He offered her the wooden box. "Please."

She used her gargantuan hands to open his precious box. "It's empty, sir. Were you looking for a charm or good luck piece to fit in here? I have some very nice talismans."

"No! I want the blue balls back and I want them now." The few other customers rushed out the door.

"I'm sorry, sir, about your, um, *blue ball* situation, but we don't carry sex toys here." The old biddy turned her nose up and began dusting the glass case.

"You sold me this. I want another one. Do you have another wooden box under the counter? I'll pay whatever you ask." Gus wept, begging her to acknowledge him.

"Oh, you want one of my wooden boxes. Why didn't you just say so?" Her dangly earrings made music as she bent to retrieve a wooden box much like the first one. Relief gushed through him.

"That will be one thousand dollars." She held out her palm, waiting. Gus paid without protest and ran to his car, box in hand.

He made himself wait until he got home to open the wooden box. This meant 100 more chances and he wouldn't waste them as he had before. He'd schedule his orgasms this time. Heck, he would go out on dates and have real sex to prolong using his balls. It wasn't like he didn't know how to socialize when he needed to.

Plan made, Gus sat on the side of the bed, holding his most precious commodity. "I'll just take a peek before I put it in the drawer."

He opened the box and found...a fortune cookie. Puzzled, he cracked it open. Inside was a small slip of paper that read, *Take her to dinner you dumb bastard!*

Gus threw the fortune into the bedside table drawer and pulled out a little black book, rubbing his balls and then shifting them a bit. He dialed the first number on the page.

"Hello, Gina?"

BLAKE
EATS OUT

Shoshanna Evers

Victoria was glad the restaurant was packed. It meant the food should be as good as the reviews claimed.

"Right this way," the hostess said, leading her and Blake through a crowded path of tables situated too close together.

She'd wanted to fuck him before they went out, to sit on his face for a good hour or so and relax. But they'd made the reservations over a month ago, and places such as this one in Manhattan weren't always easy to get into.

So she'd had to delay her sexual release—despite having him greet her at the door naked, kneeling, in his collar. A lovely sight to see after a long day of work...calling her authors, editing manuscripts, and meeting with one of her favorite literary agents for lunch.

There just hadn't been enough time to use him the way he loved to be used—for her pleasure alone.

"May we have that booth in the back?" Victoria asked, and slid the hostess a tip before she could protest that the booth was meant for a larger party.

"Yes, ma'am, I think we can arrange that." The hostess smiled and they followed.

Victoria wanted the seclusion of the leather-upholstered red circular booth, where she and her slave could enjoy themselves properly.

Blake took her coat and draped it neatly next to him, helping her slide in across the leather, and the hostess departed.

"Thank you, Little Blake."

He raised his eyebrows at her use of his pet name, the name she reserved for when they were alone together. When he was wearing his collar and not much else. His dark, shaggy hair fell into his eyes and she smiled.

"It's my pleasure, Mistress," he murmured.

God, he was so cute. Absolutely adorable, and all hers.

Victoria took her house keys from her purse and rolled them in her hand, enjoying the expression on his handsome young face. Enjoyed making him wonder what she was going to do, here, now.

At the restaurant.

With a manipulated clumsy gesture, she let the keys fall from her fingers and under the table.

"Get the keys."

Blake obeyed immediately, ducking beneath the table. But when he started to rise, she stopped him with a pinch to his lean, muscular shoulder.

And so he remained under the table as the waiter approached them.

"What can I get you?" the man asked. He wasn't nearly as sweet and subservient as Blake had been when she first met him, when he'd waited on her at the diner. Too bad.

"My partner forgot something, but he'll be back. In the mean-time, I'd like to order just for myself. I don't know how long he'll be gone, and I'm starving for something...satisfying."

"Sounds good," the waiter said, and took her order of a carafe of red wine and grilled chicken.

When he was gone, Victoria put her hand under the table, tangling her fingers in Blake's hair. He didn't say a word when she pulled his hair sharply, but she could tell by his shoulders that he'd arranged himself on his knees, the way he normally did at her feet.

"Too bad Blake won't get to eat anything tonight," she said quietly, as if to herself. "Then again, he does need to eat *something.*"

At her words, she could practically feel his grin from under the table.

He maneuvered his body between her legs. She wasn't wearing any underwear underneath her skirt, and already her pussy dampened at the thought of him readying himself to service her.

The waiter returned with her wine, and she smiled and thanked him as she pressed her stiletto heel into the tender flesh of Blake's ass—at least it felt like where his ass was, based on how her legs were positioned.

No sound. The boy was good.

She took a deep sip of the wine, letting it wash away her day, and willed herself to relax into the moment. After all, she had a very willing slave between her legs, ready to spend as much time as necessary to pleasure her.

For all he knew, her pussy would be his only meal this evening. The thought made her smile.

Blake reached tentatively between her legs, running his strong hands along the sensitive skin on her inner thighs. A shudder of desire coursed through her, but she focused on the wine, taking another sip.

Now. Lick me now.

But he was taking his sweet time, carefully spreading her nether lips, stroking her clit with his fingers. Did he deserve another pinch?

And then, his mouth. Hot and wet, his tongue covered her shaved pussy, licking her slowly.

Another sip of wine.

Everything about the moment aroused her. The public place, the unaware patrons mere feet away from them, and the feel of his hair tickling the inside of her thighs.

She inhaled sharply and pulled her phone out, scrolling through her email so that she wouldn't look strange sitting by herself. There was no way to keep her face completely neutral, not with his mouth on her pussy, his lips pressing against— *Ahh fuck yeah*—and so she pretended to be working while she waited for her food.

This time, when the waiter returned, she pressed her heel into Blake even harder, willing him to keep going, keep going. He did, and the waiter served her the chicken and left.

The fork slipped from her grasp as Blake sucked her clit into his mouth, gently nibbling it, giving her everything he had.

But she lifted her silverware again and cut her food, sliding a piece of chicken in a delicious sauce past her lips.

"That tastes so good," she murmured. "I wish Blake could taste this."

He responded by licking her with even more fervor, her thighs spread beneath the tablecloth, held apart with his hands, and she pinched him to remind him to slow down, to take his time.

After all, the meal was quite good. She had a lot of emails to answer. She could be there for a while until the appropriate time for Blake to "return" from his absence presented itself.

The thought of Blake under the table, not knowing how long he'd be there, locked between her thighs, brought on a wave of pleasure, and she closed her legs around him, holding him in place.

He licked her the way she'd trained him, with reverence and hunger, and she came hard, silently, controlling herself so that she wouldn't give away their game.

She poured another glass of wine and took another sip. Delicious.

Every meal should be like this, she mused.

Blake waited patiently at her feet while she ate a few more bites of her meal, letting her sensitive post-climactic clit take a moment, before she ran her fingers through his hair, lightly scraping her nails across his scalp and along his ears.

How was he doing, during all of this? With a slight movement, as if crossing her legs or shifting her weight, Victoria slid one stiletto off and ran her naked foot over his muscular leg, until she found his cock.

He was so hard it had to be painful. The thought appealed.

She slowly, tortuously, rubbed her foot against the rigid length, just long enough to feel his breath panting desperately against her pussy, and then she stopped.

Blake pressed a kiss to the inside of her thigh, and she smiled. He must want to come so badly, but it didn't matter. Tonight was about her. And since it pleased her, she'd torture his hard cock as much as she wanted to without letting him come.

Very carefully, she slipped her heel back on, and ran the sharp stiletto along his cock, letting Blake feel her power over him.

"We're not done," she said softly, so only he could hear, and pinched his shoulder again.

He took the cue and went back at it, licking her clit with a longing so intense she had to force herself to eat her meal while he sucked her or she'd come again too quickly.

Her muscles quivered as he continued, an enormous pressure building within her until she climaxed, holding Blake so tightly with her legs she imagined she was cutting off his oxygen supply.

When he'd drawn out every last moment of her orgasm, she took another sip of wine, and checked the time on her phone. She looked around. No one was looking their way.

"Okay," she said, and gave him a playful kick.

"I found the keys, Ma'am," Blake said as he slid back up into the booth, holding them in his hand. His hair was disheveled, and he looked like the college kid he was. Adorable.

And all hers.

"Oh yes," she smiled. "You most definitely did."

FAMOUS LAST WORDS

Tenille Brown

'm tired of kissing your ass!"

Ralph was pulling his black T-shirt down over his flat, fuzzy abdomen, his gray eyes scanning the room for his belongings.

They were ugly words coming from such sexy lips, but Macy wasn't surprised. Ralph was quick tempered just like she was, which was probably why they weren't going to make it for the long haul.

Macy first folded her lips, and then she bit down on them hard. She wanted to tell Ralph that she had never asked him to kiss her ass and she wouldn't let him do it now, anyway, but she didn't want to give him the satisfaction of a response.

As she stood in the bedroom, Macy's ass was naked and chilly, as they had been in the middle of a pretty good fuck when the argument started.

One wrong word was all it took—that's all it ever took with Macy—and she was storming out of the bedroom in a rage.

She didn't care *who* didn't get their orgasm.

"Sometimes, I swear, Macy, you're just not worth the trouble," he had said in the middle of sliding his cock between her hungry lips.

All because she had asked him to shift a little, and lean back a little more, and that had been it. Ralph had gone from zero to one hundred in an instant.

And Macy let him. Now she stepped aside and opened the door for him.

She said, "Get the fuck out, Ralph."

Ralph opened his mouth, and then he closed it again. Then he walked out, the buckle on his still loosened jeans clanging loudly.

Ralph was a drummer Macy had met at an indie concert during the summer and to both her surprise and his, he had managed to stick around five months. But today he had just walked his last walk with her.

Before Ralph, of course, there had been Juan, and before that, Sly.

But every time, they had done something, they had all done or said something to fuck it all up.

Some people said Macy's patience was short, or she was too choosy, or nitpicky, but Macy knew that she was simply a no-nonsense type of girl. On her own in New York City since the age of nineteen, she'd had no choice.

Now, at twenty-seven, Macy had made her way in this city and no way was she turning back.

She didn't need a man's money. She had her job at the bookstore for that. She didn't need his dick. She had an impressive collection of vibrators for that. She didn't even need the company.

Macy was just fine, and she had every intention of remaining that way.

For emphasis, Macy pushed the door closed with all her

might so that it slammed hard behind him, then she flung her tired, bare ass onto the sofa.

And it was in that moment between the door swinging shut and Macy hearing that telltale click and her ass making contact with the firm pillows of her chair that she realized that Ralph had forgotten something.

And she had forgotten something.

They had forgotten something. And it rested just inside the shallow cavity of her curvy, white ass.

It wasn't foreign to Macy to fuck on the last day of the relationship. It was simply breakup sex. But she hadn't actually planned to dump Ralph today, which was why she let him do that...that *thing* in the first place.

Sure she had been curious, too, and she had rather enjoyed it, but Ralph had made the mistake of talking before they were completely finished and before she knew it, Macy had blown her top and asked him to leave.

Now she was stuck in her apartment alone, with a ten-inch string of pearls tucked inside her ass.

It was funny how the pearls weren't that uncomfortable until now; she wasn't as blatantly aware of their presence until she was stuck alone with them.

Macy knew the beads were harmless enough, but suddenly she felt as if she were sitting on a stick of dynamite. One tug and they'd explode.

Which meant she couldn't exactly run down the stairs and chase after him. She couldn't even imagine walking the ten or so feet to her bedroom to try to do it herself.

Of course, if she *could* do it herself, she could do so right here in her own living room, but she couldn't. They were wedged pretty far. Macy knew, because she had specifically asked for it that way.

She had been looking forward to the sensation of having them pulled from between her cheeks, the feeling of each bead popping through her anus as Ralph gently tugged.

Macy had to do something. She was getting worried now.

So she picked up the telephone and dialed Ralph's number.

"What?" Ralph asked.

And his voice was cold, colder than Macy had ever had ever heard it before. She was tempted to hang up the phone, but she was reminded by the tingling at the base of her anus that she couldn't do that just yet.

"Hi," Macy said. "I just wanted to call and apologize."

Ralph sighed. "Fuck that, Macy, you never apologize. Not for shit. Now, what in the hell do you want? I left your key on the fucking counter, if that's the reason."

"No, it's not that, Ralph. I..."

"I'm hanging up now, Macy."

"No!" Macy screamed into the phone. "Ralph, we forgot about the goddamned beads!"

"This was supposed to be fun."

Macy said this as she got into position, leaning over the back of her love seat.

"It is fun, for me. Well, funny, that is," Ralph said.

There Macy was biting her tongue again. She couldn't say what she wanted to say, not until these beads were out of her ass and Ralph was out of her apartment.

She was only naked from the waist down, but she felt as if her tanned body were fully exposed to her newly ex-boyfriend.

"Spread your legs," Ralph said.

Macy looked back over her shoulder at Ralph. "What?"

Ralph sucked his teeth. "You have to spread 'em. You know how this works, Macy."

Macy pushed her legs apart, propping herself up on her elbows.

"Now try and relax, because since you hate me now, it probably won't feel as good as it would have."

She knew Ralph was relishing standing there over her, knowing he had the power and all the control over her. She didn't have many friends, and especially none that she trusted enough to pull anything out of her ass.

So Macy had to stifle it all just this once, until Ralph did what she needed.

Ralph started with the first two beads, which gave Macy such a sense of relief that her exhale blew the hair away from her face.

"Is it wrong of me to want to know how it feels?" Ralph asked.

Macy could have sworn his voice had gone soft, as if he was trying to sound sexy or something.

Her patience was wearing thin, but she was in a rather compromising...*position*. "No, Ralph, I suppose it wouldn't be so wrong."

"Well, then," Ralph said, "tell me."

Macy thought for a while. Then she answered, "It feels relieving and relaxing."

"And what else?'

"And painful and pleasant."

"And?"

"And I want it to be over, but I don't." Macy was mindlessly grinding now, her elbows and knees digging into the cushions.

Ralph gently tugged, releasing one bead at a time.

"I can tell you what it looks like, if you want to know," Ralph said, still tugging.

"Go on. Tell me."

"They look small and shiny slipping from between your cheeks. Your ass looks round and perfect holding on to the dangling string."

"You always did exaggerate. And for the record, no one will ever mistake you for a poet."

"Duly noted," Ralph said and he added, "We're almost there."

Macy briefly questioned the word "we," but when Ralph accidentally brushed up against her thigh, she suddenly realized what he meant.

Macy was wet and Ralph was hard.

And coinciding with this realization came the exit of the final bead from Macy's anus. Her knees buckled in an unfamiliar mixture of pleasure and relief.

Ralph handed her the wet, white strand of pearls. Macy looked at them strangely before she took them from him and tossed them on the cushion.

"What?" Macy asked when she noticed him lingering.

"One for the road?" Ralph asked, while reaching up to pull her damp hair away from her freckled face.

Macy shrugged as nonchalantly as she could and said, "Sure, why not?"

After all it was just breakup sex, just Ralph stripping off his clothes and lying her across the love seat facedown to fuck her from behind.

However, it was no ordinary fuck. It was no doggy-style romp. From the feel of things, Ralph was going to fuck Macy in the ass.

She found herself biting into the velvety material when he entered her, and clenching her eyes shut as she tried not to tighten up around his cock.

Macy might have let herself be more vulnerable if she didn't detest him so much in this moment. She became angry again thinking about the way he spoke to her and the ugly words he used.

The angrier Macy became, the harder she pushed her ass against Ralph's cock. She pushed back so hard on her knees that she knocked Ralph nearly off balance and he reached out to hold on to the back of the chair.

Ralph smacked her on the side of her hip. "Still mad, eh?"

"Fuck you," Macy managed as her body began to vibrate.

"No, fuck you," Ralph said, and pushed his cock in farther.

Macy couldn't recall a sweeter pain. She couldn't remember a time when she wanted to come so bad and had to work so hard to hold it back.

Following some sort of twisted instinct, Ralph reached down and around and placed his fingers on Macy's cunt. He began viciously pressing and rubbing against her clit while he continued to ass-fuck her.

Macy bit down on her pillow, her expensive pillow that she had almost thrown at Ralph before he walked out the door.

She was coming and she couldn't wait. She grabbed on to the arm of the love seat, pressing her fingers so firmly into the material that her knuckles turned red.

Ralph laughed that stupid laugh of his.

"I feel you all over my fingers," he said. Then, "It's okay because here I come, too...."

Ralph burst steaming lava inside of her ass. There was so much that it leaked onto her cheeks and streamed slowly down the backs of her thighs.

"What a fuck of a lay," Ralph exhaled, and got up to get dressed.

"By the way," Macy said. "If you did want to kiss my ass, that would have been your one and only chance because you'll never see it again."

Ralph shook his head slowly as he opened the door.

He said, "You've got the best ass I've ever seen in my life, Macy. But, I swear, it's not worth the trouble."

"Go to hell!" Macy said, and slammed the door shut in his face.

OBJECTS OF DESIRE

Annabeth Leong

S amantha talked about shoving household objects up her cunt when she needed to get Brandon off quickly. When they fucked late at night, blurry and achy in the eyes, her made-up account of sticking a rolling pin inside herself could transform his dutiful, habitual motions to urgent, explosive thrusts.

She thought she was merely inventing those stories for him, until she noticed the world changing around her. Everywhere she went, everything she touched became a cock. In doctors' waiting rooms, she speculated about whether she could fuck herself with rolled-up magazines. In the hardware store, thick-handled tools left her weak in the knees. In the grocery store, she measured vegetables with hands and eyes, her mind wandering far outside the relative norm of cucumbers into the dangerous, prickly territory of brussels sprouts still attached to the branch and unpeeled artichokes.

She took these thoughts home for Brandon, of course, but they rumbled around inside Samantha as well.

Then she caught herself remembering. In college, when she felt too ashamed to buy a vibrator, she used to attempt to satisfy herself with a brush handle or a bottle of shampoo, squatting furtively in the dormitory shower to avoid gasping her pleasure where her roommate could hear. Once, her cunt had swallowed a new bar of soap whole with one smooth, alarming ripple of muscle. Samantha's heart had pounded then as she stuck fingers inside herself, desperate to fish it out. Still, if she was honest, the thought of being caught, of having to waddle to a phone to call for help with her cunt stuffed full, had thrilled her as much as it mortified her.

Not long after the soap incident, fear of hurting herself with improvised dildos forced Samantha to summon the courage to purchase a Magic Wand. She had forgotten the delicious shame she felt when she got desperate enough to fuck herself with whatever was available.

Now, trembling with the fantasies she'd reawakened by whispering to Brandon, Samantha realized she missed the dirty risks she used to take. She missed seeing if something could fit, if she could force it in despite an odd texture or protrusion. She missed being surprised, whether by pleasure or pain or both.

"I want to do it for real," she told Brandon late one night, while he worked his cock in and out of her. "You can watch." His ass jerked hard on his next thrust. His angular, shadowed face clenched tight, and he came.

Brandon collapsed against Samantha's neck, spouting apologies. She held up a hand to stop the flood of guilt. No time for that in the face of practical considerations. "Thank god tomorrow is Saturday," she said. "I'm going to need a while. I'm going to fuck the whole damn kitchen."

It didn't matter then that Brandon had a few beers in him from the bar they'd visited that night. As Samantha described what she planned to do, his cock snaked longer inside her and got hard again. Samantha rolled them over so she could ride him. She listed kitchen utensils until they both came.

The next afternoon, Samantha sat Brandon in a chair in the corner of the kitchen and told him to stay still and be quiet. He frowned, the sharpness of his handsome features growing more pronounced. She kissed him rather than saying more, letting her mouth linger against his. She traced the shape of his jaw with her fingers. When she stood back, he gave her a lazy, heavy-lidded smile that absolved her of selfishness.

She had been more open with Brandon than with anyone, but this thing had to be wordless. He might think she wanted to do this for him, and she could let him. Really, she allowed him to watch as a thank-you for reawakening this old desire of hers. And she wanted a witness. Then, later, she could think about how someone else had seen her horny for the strangest cock of all, and shiver with shame. She didn't want to deal with him right now—not with his feelings, or whatever he might desire.

Samantha began by setting lube and condoms on the kitchen table. Older and wiser than her college self, she planned to mitigate the risks of shoving random objects up her pussy. She turned the lights down low and started up a mellow, bluesy playlist. Right now, she wanted to make herself forget Brandon was even in the room.

She stripped down to a camisole, no bra, and a pair of panties. Then she scanned the kitchen. Her eye first fell on a container full of cooking tools—spatulas, a potato masher, a whisk and a meat tenderizer.

She took this back to the table and shoved her panties down until they tangled around her ankles. She lay down flat on her

back with her legs spread and her feet propped up on the slats
of one of the chairs.

The potato masher's handle flared with an appealing curve.
Samantha rolled a condom over it and smeared the end with
lube.

Her cunt practically smacked its lips, she'd already gotten
so wet. The handle slurped into her, long and a little too thin,
and much cooler than skin. It didn't feel as good as a cock or
a dildo, but that only emphasized how inappropriate it was to
slide it inside herself. Samantha shuddered, her muscles fluttering around the foreign object. She pushed it in as deep as
it could go, gripping the business end of the masher and stirring the handle inside herself as if her cunt juices were a thick
stew. She wondered what would happen if she pushed it in even
farther, about how badly it might hurt to force herself to take
more length than her body could stand.

In seconds, her every muscle tightened and her breathing
changed. Just a little twitch, a little brush against her G-spot,
and she would have come right then. Orgasmic spasms hovered
at the corners of her vision, but Samantha fought them, her hands
freezing the masher in place. She didn't want this yet. Satisfaction now was the enemy. Samantha wanted to foster genuine
desperation, the way she used to feel when she resorted to whatever vaguely phallic objects she could find. She wanted to be
willing to fuck just about anything that might make her come.

It was a calculated risk. She'd learned over the years that if
she didn't take an opportunity to come when it presented itself,
her body seemed to freeze up a little, no longer able to nudge
itself over the precipice once she'd pulled back. Denying herself
now, it could be an hour or more before she could work herself
to the same level of excitement.

Samantha yanked the potato masher out of her cunt, afraid

she couldn't continue to resist temptation. She traced its slicked handle over the tops of her thighs, teased her clit for just one dangerous second, then worked her way up to toy with the bottom of her camisole. It left a sticky, pungent trail of lube combined with her own arousal.

Samantha flipped the masher over and tried kneading her breasts with it. She pressed it against herself hard enough that its wavy pattern pinched a little even through the camisole. She pushed the garment up to bare her breasts and repeated the gesture.

It felt nice, but it definitely cooled off the threatening orgasm. Samantha's body still hummed with arousal, but she felt the entrenched inner resistance that followed attempts at control. It would be hard to come now, and so she could turn herself into a panting, horny mess.

She cast the potato masher aside in favor of the meat tenderizer. The weight of the metal object forced her to change her grip. She pressed it where the masher had been, sliding its nubby surface over her nipples, relishing the way it hurt a little. She wanted more.

The whisk wouldn't do to put inside herself, but she liked the way it rattled when she picked it up. Samantha let her legs fall outward into a butterfly pose and slapped it once against her inner thigh. Its metal loops made precise, stinging contact with her sensitive flesh. She squeezed her eyes shut and rocked as the sensation rippled through her. She liked the idea of what that would do to her clit, but it would be a struggle to actually hit herself there.

She feinted toward her pussy with the whisk, but chickened out at the last moment and brought it down on her thigh again instead. From the corner, Brandon spoke up. "Do you want me to—"

She brandished the meat tenderizer at him. "I told you to be quiet."

Already, interacting with him threatened to break the spell she'd been building. She channeled her irritation into her next strike and this time made definite contact with her arousal-swollen clit. Pain flashed through her, but the whisk vibrated from the blow, and sympathetic trembling penetrated deep into her pelvis, to the subterranean parts of her clit that only the most powerful sensations could reach.

She gritted her teeth and tried the move again. She yelped and writhed away each time, but the blows landed, as if some diabolical other self drove her hand.

Brandon groaned. From the corner of her eye, Samantha saw he'd taken out his cock. Good. That should keep him busy.

She switched tools, allowing the whisk to clatter to the floor. The metal spatula she replaced it with whistled through the air and landed with terrifying force. Samantha went still, holding the cold metal tight against her clit. She ached inside. She needed something to touch her there, so high in her cunt it practically reached her guts.

She set the utensils aside and sat up fast enough to make her head spin. The kitchen chair she'd braced against tipped over and crashed. She jumped up to right it, then paused, her hand closing around one of its legs. She wanted it.

Another condom, more lube, and she was ready to take this, too. She turned the chair from side to side, searching for the best angle. Finally, she dropped to all fours in front of it and backed onto it, the square-shaped wooden leg parting her cunt lips.

It was thick enough that it resisted slipping straight in, even with the lube. The chair slid backward across the floor. Samantha shot her foot out to catch and anchor it, then tried again. She pushed the leg as far in as she dared, aware of its remaining length but afraid of hurting herself. The chair leg angled up, rubbing her G-spot as she began to fuck herself against it. She moaned long and loud. She lifted one hand to rub her clit as she took the chair leg, but this put too much weight on her other hand. She grunted in frustration.

Now, she wanted to come. She liked the image of herself fucking the chair leg. She wanted her cunt to pulse around its hard wooden edges. She wanted to slip a little while in the throes of ecstasy and wind up with it nestled into her to the point of pain. Samantha shoved back harder. She squeezed her muscles and deliberately pressed until she had to suck air in between her teeth.

It was no use. She'd gotten so wet she couldn't feel the leg in the places she needed to get friction—not around her entrance, or along the sides of her inner walls. Its delicious pressure got her ready for more, but the leg itself could not deliver.

Her decision to hold off her orgasm had come back to bite her, and she began to regret it. Would it have been so terrible to fuck the chair leg while aftershocks quivered through her cunt?

She rocked faster, hurt herself a little more, but Samantha could tell this wouldn't work. She needed something thicker inside her, something she could really clench around. Whining in the back of her throat, she pushed off the chair. She kicked it out of the way, enjoying the violence of the gesture.

Samantha scanned the kitchen again, looking for something else to fuck. She could see Brandon's cock pulsing from the corner of her eye, but right now she didn't want to fuck her boyfriend or anything that would clearly fit in a vagina. She wanted to stretch, to fuck an object, something that would make her feel dirty and a little ashamed, something that scared her.

Her gaze fell on the rolling pin tucked behind a set of

nonstick pans. The story she'd told Brandon flowed into her mind in a rush.

She seized the rolling pin in a fit of lust, its thickness in her palm dropping a thrill of fear into the pit of her belly. She didn't know if getting it inside her was at all possible or just a fantasy, but she had to try.

Samantha lay on the table again. At some point, she'd started sweating, and the wooden surface felt cold against her sticky back. She worked big handfuls of lube into her cunt until she couldn't have gotten traction on her clit if she'd tried. She snapped a condom over the rolling pin, slipping it over the thin rod at the end, then spreading its base wide to get it over the thicker roller. She took a deep breath and tested it.

The rolling pin was heavy, hard to hold up with one hand. The rod slid into her easily, but the roller itself seemed impossibly thick. Her pulse sped as she explored herself with the handle and felt the roller probe at her entrance. Now, she fantasized about Brandon, imagining him rising from his chair in the corner and taking heavy, impatient steps toward where she lay. With one hand he would hold her down, and with the other he would force the roller past her body's resistance until she lay gasping and stunned, more full inside than she'd ever been in her life.

Samantha moaned aloud at the image and spread her legs as wide as she could, bracing them on the edges of the table. She bore down with her cunt muscles on the roller and gripped the utensil with both hands, trying to drive it into herself.

The pressure it placed on her entrance was just the sort of thing she'd been looking for—except she needed more. Samantha pulled the rolling pin out and spread her cunt lips as wide as she could with the fingers of one hand. Unfortunately, when she repositioned it to push in, her own fingers were in the way.

Samantha almost sobbed with frustration. She squirmed on the table, struggling to open her legs even more. When she made no progress there, she closed her legs a little and used her thighs to prop up the rolling pin so she could use both hands to work it in.

She reached between her legs and tugged her cunt open, trying to wrap herself around the thick roller. She fit one side in, then lost ground when she tried to fit in the other.

She held herself half-lifted, the awkward position dictated by her need to manipulate her cunt until it took the rolling pin. Sweat poured from her neck onto her chest, then slid down to her stomach. She felt hot and smelly. Her fingers skidded over her clit and labia, too lubed up to gain any purchase against her recalcitrant body.

From his corner, Brandon gave a strangled cry as his cock shot come onto his chest. Samantha responded with desperate irritation. Of course he'd come from watching her display, while she still writhed, helpless with lust for this damned monster of a rolling pin. She felt convinced that she would not be able to come without getting it inside her body. She was too slippery and numb everywhere except for where it counted—everywhere except the exquisitely sensitive ring of flesh and muscle just at the entrance to her vagina, where she and the rolling pin had become locked in a pitched battle.

Samantha needed it to penetrate her, and yet it had no give. It would not compromise any bit of its hard thickness, would not compress in response to her squeezing the way flesh would. Utterly implacable in its challenge, it made her desire it all the more.

She gripped it again with both hands, flung her head back and lifted her hips as high as they would go. She relaxed into the pain of the thing straining her opening, and held it in place until she couldn't breathe. She shook her head from side to side, growling and sweating.

Then it came, that alarming involuntary ripple of muscle she remembered from the time her cunt had swallowed the bar of soap. Slowly, inexorably, the rolling pin sank into her cunt. White light flickered over Samantha's eyelids and she screamed her agonizing pleasure.

The spasms that started a moment later were ecstatic torment as well. Her stuffed cunt, stretched to capacity, had nothing left to give, and yet her muscles forced the skin to undulate around the unforgiving thickness of the roller.

As soon as she could bear to, Samantha unclenched her hands from the rolling pin and let it fall. Aching everywhere, she sought Brandon's eyes, expecting to see disgust on his face, or fear at the power of her orgasm around something other than his cock. Coming down now, she no longer wanted shame. It took all her courage to meet his gaze.

All she saw in him was awe, the very sentiment that spread through her own body with every pulsating aftershock.

ABOUT THE AUTHORS

JACQUELINE APPLEBEE (writing-in-shadows.co.uk) is a British writer who breaks down barriers with smut. Her stories have appeared in publications including *Best Women's Erotica*, *Best Lesbian Erotica*, *Penthouse* and *DIVA* magazine. Jacqueline hopes to write a best-selling novel so she can live in a lighthouse with a few adoring fans.

PRESTON AVERY (PrestonAvery.com) resides merrily by the sea, working and living with only slightly less than reckless abandon. She loves reading almost as much as writing and is featured in the anthologies *The Big Book of Orgasm*, *Geek Love* and *Morning, Noon, and Night*.

ERZABET BISHOP has had a love affair with books since she first started reading. Just recently, she discovered that writing naughty stories was even more fun. She lives with her husband, a menagerie of dogs and a mountain of books she is sure will crush her one day in her sleep.

LOUISE BLAYDON writes erotic romance of various kinds from the house she shares in Oxfordshire, England, with three cats and a lot of fortifying coffee.

HARPER BLISS writes lesbian erotica. She's had short stories published in anthologies by Xcite Books, House of Erotica and Storm Moon Press. She is the author of the *High Rise* series and several other novelettes and novellas for Ladylit.

RACHEL KRAMER BUSSEL (rachelkramerbussel.com) has edited over forty anthologies, including *Only You: Erotic Romance for Women, Orgasmic, Fast Girls, Women in Lust, Gotta Have It, The Mile High Club*, and the *Best Bondage Erotica* and *Best Sex Writing* series. She writes widely about sex, dating, food, books and pop culture.

HEIDI CHAMPA (heidichampa.blogspot.com) has been published in numerous anthologies including *Best Women's Erotica 2010, Irresistible, Best Erotic Romance 2012 & 2013* and *Sweet Confessions*. She has also steamed up the pages of *Bust* magazine.

KYOKO CHURCH's short stories have been published in anthologies by Black Lace, Rubicund Publishing and Xcite Books. Book One, *Nymphomania,* and Book Two, *Sapphic Secrets,* in her *Draper Estate Trilogy* were published by Xcite in 2012. *For Her Pleasure* was published by HarperCollins Mischief in February 2013.

MONICA CORWIN (monicacorwin.com) is a military analyst turned romance and erotica author. In addition to numerous works across various publishers Monica is the founder of *The*

Bibliophilic Book Blog and a former columnist for *Night Owl Magazine.*

When **MADISON EINHART** isn't writing, she's either covered in acrylic paint or falling in love (again) with her piano keys. Writing has been her longtime love affair—after coming to her senses, she's decided it's time to share that love with the world.

BEATRIX ELLROY is an ex-librarian book hound with a love of words, the dirtier the better. A newcomer to erotica, her previous work has included everything from articles about computer games to literary fiction, but filthy fiction is her passion and her weakness.

BLAIR EROTICA is a traveling writer who focuses on the erotic and passionate. Blair has published stories online in Freeflash-fiction.com and *Bare Back Magazine,* a novella with House of Erotica and has had several short pieces included in anthologies that explore the driving forces that make us human and interesting.

SHOSHANNA EVERS (ShoshannaEvers.com) has over two dozen novels and stories published, including the *Enslaved Trilogy* from Simon & Schuster's Pocket Star, and the best-selling erotica *Dominatrix Fantasy Trilogy.* Shoshanna also hit #1 on the Authorship, Erotica Writing, and Romance Writing Amazon Bestseller lists. Forthcoming is the postapocalyptic *Pulse Trilogy.*

LUCY FELTHOUSE (lucyfelthouse.co.uk) writes erotica and erotic romance in a variety of subgenres and pairings, and has over seventy publications to her name, with many more in the pipeline. These include stories in *Best Bondage Erotica 2012* and *2013*, and *Best Women's Erotica 2013*.

Erotic writer **TAMSIN FLOWERS** (tamsinflowers.com) is as keen to entertain her readers as she is to explore every aspect of female (and male) erotica. Her short stories can be found in anthologies from Xcite Books, House of Erotica and Cleis Press and she is currently working on a number of novels and novellas.

TILLY HUNTER is a British author and newspaper journalist with a wicked imagination and a fondness for stories of outdoor pursuits, healthy living and BDSM. Her work has been published by Xcite Books and the websites Every Night Erotica and Oysters & Chocolate.

JOANNE KENRICK is a multi-published author who writes both contemporaries and paranormals. Her *Irish Kisses* series earned her the title of an Amazon bestselling author, and she regularly blogs with The Pop Culture Divas, Diamond Authors and Paranormal Romantics.

HILARY KEYES is an art aficionado and punk rocker living in Japan. She's into design, tattoos, kimonos, decadent history and dressing up her plastic anatomy skeleton, Hiroshi-kun.

ANNABETH LEONG (annabethleong.blogspot.com) has written erotica of many flavors—dark, romantic, kinky, vanilla, straight, lesbian, bi and ménage. She believes the kitchen beats out the bedroom as the most erotic room in the house. Her work has been published by Cleis, Xcite, Circlet, Coming Together and others.

MEDEA MOR (medeamor.blogspot.com) has had short stories published by Cleis, Mischief and Xcite, and hopes soon to start self-publishing longer works of fiction. She specializes in BDSM-flavored erotica with wicked, charismatic doms and intelligent, well-educated subs.

ANIKA RAY's erotic stories have appeared in several anthologies, most recently *Sweet Confessions*, edited by Violet Blue, and *Best Women's Erotica 2013*. She works as a foreign correspondent.

Erotica writer **GISELLE RENARDE** is a queer Canadian, avid volunteer, contributor to more than one hundred short-story anthologies and author of numerous electronic and print books, including *Anonymous*, *Nanny State* and *My Mistress' Thighs*. Ms. Renarde lives across from a park, with two bilingual cats who sleep on her head.

COLE RILEY is the pen name for a well-known journalist and reviewer. His work has appeared in several anthologies and magazines, including a recent stint as a columnist at *SexIs Magazine*. He has edited two popular anthologies, *Making the Hook-Up: Edgy Sex with Soul* and *Too Much Boogie: Erotic Remixes of the Dirty Blues*.

MIEL ROSE is a rural queer femme, magic maker, and healer. You can find her other sexy stories in a multitude of anthologies including: *Lesbian Lust*, *The Harder She Comes* and the forthcoming *Leather Ever After*. Or look for her self-published collection, *Overflow: Tales of Butch-Femme Love, Sex and Desire*.

KISSA STARLING (kissastarling.com) began penning notes in class many years ago. Around 2007 she began writing with the intent to publish. A Christmas contest caught her eye, and she hasn't stopped submitting since. Her stories have appeared in a few Cleis anthologies including *Peep Show*, *Please, Sir* and *Serving Him*.

SOPHIA VALENTI (sophiavalenti.blogspot.com) is the author of *Indecent Desires*, an erotic novella of spanking and submission. Her fiction has appeared in a variety of anthologies, including *Sudden Sex: 69 Sultry Short Stories*, *The Big Book of Bondage* and *Kiss My Ass*.

ALLISON WONDERLAND (aisforallison.blogspot.com) is on the write track. Her cliterature appears in *Sudden Sex*, *Best Lesbian Romance 2013*, *Sweet Love: Erotic Fantasies for Couples* and *Wild Girls, Wild Nights*. Allison has been a smutty storyteller since 2007, and her specialtease—er, specialties—are erotic romance and lesbian erotica.

ABOUT
THE EDITOR

TENILLE BROWN is a Southern wife, mother and writer. Her erotica has been featured over the past ten years online and in over fifty print and eBook anthologies including *Best Women's Erotica 2004, Chocolate Flava 1* and *3, Curvy Girls, Going Down, Best Bondage Erotica 2011* and *2012, Sapphic Planet, Suite Encounters, Open, Best Lesbian Erotica 2013, Only You, How to Write Erotic Fiction, Sudden Sex, Smut Alfresco, Smut for Chocoholics, Baby Got Back* and *Smut by the Sea Volume 2*. She contributes to Mischief Books erotic collections, the most recent being *Take Me* and *Thrill Seekers*, and has nonfiction included in *The Greenwood Encyclopedia of African American Writers*. Tenille blogs at therealtenille.com and tweets @TheRealTenille.

Many More than Fifty Shades of Erotica

Happy Endings Forever and Ever

Dark Secret Love
A Story of Submission
By Alison Tyler

Inspired by her own BDSM exploits and private diaries, Alison Tyler draws on twenty-five years of penning sultry stories to create a scorchingly hot work of fiction, a memoir-inspired novel with reality at its core. A modern-day *Story of O*, a *9 1/2 Weeks*-style journey fueled by lust, longing and the search for true love.
ISBN 978-1-57344-956-4 $16.95

High-Octane Heroes
Erotic Romance for Women
Edited by Delilah Devlin

One glance and your heart will melt—these chiseled, brave men will ignite your fantasies with their courage and charisma. Award-winning romance writer Delilah Devlin has gathered stories of hunky, red-blooded guys who enter danger zones in the name of duty, honor, country and even love.
ISBN 978-1-57344-969-4 $15.95

Duty and Desire
Military Erotic Romance
Edited by Kristina Wright

The only thing stronger than the call of duty is the call of desire. *Duty and Desire* enlists a team of hot-blooded men and women from every branch of the military who serve their country and follow their hearts.
ISBN 978-1-57344-823-9 $15.95

Smokin' Hot Firemen
Erotic Romance Stories for Women
Edited by Delilah Devlin

Delilah delivers tales of these courageous men breaking down doors to steal readers' hearts! *Smokin' Hot Firemen* imagines the romantic possibilities of being held against a massively muscled chest by a man whose mission is to save lives and serve *every* need.
ISBN 978-1-57344-934-2 $15.95

Only You
Erotic Romance for Women
Edited by Rachel Kramer Bussel

Only You is full of tenderness, raw passion, love, longing and the many emotions that kindle true romance. The couples in *Only You* test the boundaries of their love to make their relationships stronger.
ISBN 978-1-57344-909-0 $15.95

Try This at Home!

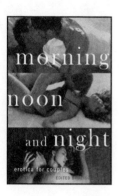

Morning, Noon and Night
Erotica for Couples
Edited by Alison Tyler

Alison Tyler thinks about sex twenty-four hours a day, and the result is *Morning, Noon and Night*, a sizzling collection of headily sensual stories featuring couples whose love fuels their lust. From delicious trysts at dawn to naughty nooners, afternoon delights and all-night-long lovemaking sessions, Alison Tyler is your guide to sultry, slippery sex.
ISBN 978-1-57344-821-5 $15.95

Anything for You
Erotica for Kinky Couples
Edited by Rachel Kramer Bussel

Whether you are a BDSM aficionado or a novice newly discovering the joys of tying up your lover, *Anything for You* will unravel a world of obsessive passion, the kind that lies just beneath the skin.
ISBN 978-1-57344-813-0 $15.95

Sweet Danger
Erotic Stories of Forbidden Desire for Couples
Edited by Violet Blue

Sweet Danger will inspire you with stories of a sexy video shoot, a rough-trade gang bang, a public sex romp served with a side of exquisite humiliation and much, much more. What is *your* deepest, most sweetly dangerous fantasy?
ISBN 978-1-57344-648-8 $14.95

Irresistible
Erotic Romance for Couples
Edited by Rachel Kramer Bussel

Irresistible features loving couples who turn their deepest fantasies into reality—resulting in uninhibited, imaginative sex they can only enjoy together.
ISBN 978-1-57344-762-1 $14.95

Sweet Confessions
Erotic Fantasies for Couples
Edited by Violet Blue

In *Sweet Confessions*, Violet Blue showcases inspirational "you can do it, too" tales that are perfect bedtime reading for lovers. The lust-inciting fantasies include spanking, exhibitionism, role-playing, three-ways and sensual adventures that will embolden real couples to reach new heights of passion.
ISBN 978-1-57344-665-5 $14.95

Unleash Your Favorite Fantasies

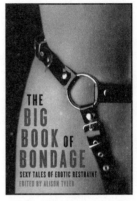

Buy 4 books, Get 1 FREE*

The Big Book of Bondage
Sexy Tales of Erotic Restraint
Edited by Alison Tyler

Nobody likes bondage more than editrix Alison Tyler, who is fascinated with the ecstasies of giving up, giving in, and entrusting one's pleasure (and pain) into the hands of another. Delve into a world of unrestrained passion, where heart-stopping dynamics will thrill and inspire you.
ISBN 978-1-57344-907-6 $15.95

Hurts So Good
Unrestrained Erotica
Edited by Alison Tyler

Intricately secured by ropes, locked in handcuffs or bound simply by a lover's command, the characters of *Hurts So Good* find themselves in the throes of pleasurable restraint in this indispensible collection by prolific, award-winning editor Alison Tyler.
ISBN 978-1-57344-723-2 $14.95

Caught Looking
Erotic Tales of Voyeurs and Exhibitionists
Edited by Alison Tyler
and Rachel Kramer Bussel

These scintillating fantasies take the reader inside a world where people get to show off, watch, and feel the vicarious thrill of sex times two, their erotic power multiplied by the eyes of another.
ISBN 978-1-57344-256-5 $14.95

Hide and Seek
Erotic Tales of Voyeurs and Exhibitionists
Edited by Rachel Kramer Bussel
and Alison Tyler

Whether putting on a deliberate show for an eager audience or peeking into the hidden sex lives of their neighbors, these show-offs and shy types go all out in their quest for the perfect peep show.
ISBN 978-1-57344-419-4 $14.95

One Night Only
Erotic Encounters
Edited by Violet Blue

"Passion and lust play by different rules in *One Night Only*. These are stories about what happens when we have just that one opportunity to ask for what we want—and we take it… Enjoy the adventure."
—Violet Blue
ISBN 978-1-57344-756-0 $14.95

Red Hot Erotic Romance

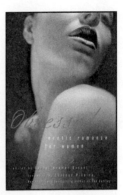

Obsessed
Erotic Romance for Women
Edited by Rachel Kramer Bussel

These stories sizzle with the kind of obsession that is fueled by our deepest desires, the ones that hold couples together, the ones that haunt us and don't let go. Whether just-blooming passions, rekindled sparks or reinvented relationships, these lovers put the object of their obsession first.
ISBN 978-1-57344-718-8 $14.95

Passion
Erotic Romance for Women
Edited by Rachel Kramer Bussel

Love and sex have always been intimately intertwined—and *Passion* shows just how delicious the possibilities are when they mingle in this sensual collection edited by award-winning author Rachel Kramer Bussel.
ISBN 978-1-57344-415-6 $14.95

Girls Who Bite
Lesbian Vampire Erotica
Edited by Delilah Devlin

Bestselling romance writer Delilah Devlin and her contributors add fresh girl-on-girl blood to the pantheon of the paranormal. The stories in *Girls Who Bite* are varied, unexpected, and soul-scorching.
ISBN 978-1-57344-715-7 $14.95

Irresistible
Erotic Romance for Couples
Edited by Rachel Kramer Bussel

This prolific editor has gathered the most popular fantasies and created a sizzling, no-holds-barred collection of explicit encounters in which couples turn their deepest desires into reality.
978-1-57344-762-1 $14.95

Heat Wave
Hot, Hot, Hot Erotica
Edited by Alison Tyler

What could be sexier or more seductive than bare, sun-warmed skin? Bestselling erotica author Alison Tyler gathers explicit stories of summer sex bursting with the sweet eroticism of swimsuits, sprinklers, and ripe strawberries.
ISBN 978-1-57344-710-2 $15.95

More from Rachel Kramer Bussel

Do Not Disturb
Hotel Sex Stories
Edited by Rachel Kramer Bussel

A delicious array of hotel hookups where it seems like anything can happen—and quite often does. "If *Do Not Disturb* were a hotel, it would be a 5-star hotel with the luxury of 24/7 entertainment available."—Erotica Revealed
978-1-57344-344-9 $14.95

Bottoms Up
Spanking Good Stories
Edited by Rachel Kramer Bussel

As sweet as it is kinky, *Bottoms Up* will propel you to pick up a paddle and share in both pleasure and pain, or perhaps simply turn the other cheek.
ISBN 978-1-57344-362-3 $15.95

Orgasmic
Erotica for Women
Edited by Rachel Kramer Bussel

What gets you off? Let *Orgasmic* count the ways...with 25 stories focused on female orgasm, there is something here for every reader.
ISBN 978-1-57344-402-6 $14.95

Please, Sir
Erotic Stories of Female Submission
Edited by Rachel Kramer Bussel

These 22 kinky stories celebrate the thrill of submission by women who know exactly what they want.
ISBN 978-1-57344-389-0 $14.95

Fast Girls
Erotica for Women
Edited by Rachel Kramer Bussel

Fast Girls celebrates the girl with a reputation, the girl who goes all the way, and the girl who doesn't know how to say "no."
ISBN 978-1-57344-384-5 $14.95

Bestselling Erotica for Couples

Sweet Life
Erotic Fantasies for Couples
Edited by Violet Blue

Your ticket to a front row seat for first-time spankings, breathtaking role-playing scenes, sex parties, women who strap it on and men who love to take it, not to mention threesomes of every combination.
ISBN 978-1-57344-133-9 $14.95

Sweet Life 2
Erotic Fantasies for Couples
Edited by Violet Blue

"This is a we-did-it-you-can-too anthology of real couples playing out their fantasies." —Lou Paget, author of *365 Days of Sensational Sex*
ISBN 978-1-57344-167-4 $15.95

Sweet Love
Erotic Fantasies for Couples
Edited by Violet Blue

"If you ever get a chance to try out your number-one fantasies in real life—and I assure you, there will be more than one—say yes. It's well worth it. May this book, its adventurous authors, and the daring and satisfied characters be your guiding inspiration."—Violet Blue
ISBN 978-1-57344-381-4 $14.95

Afternoon Delight
Erotica for Couples
Edited by Alison Tyler

"Alison Tyler evokes a world of heady sensuality where fantasies are fearlessly explored and dreams gloriously realized."
—Barbara Pizio, Executive Editor, *Penthouse Variations*
ISBN 978-1-57344-341-8 $14.95

Three-Way
Erotic Stories
Edited by Alison Tyler

"Three means more of everything. Maybe I'm greedy, but when it comes to sex, I like more. More fingers. More tongues. More limbs. More tangling and wrestling on the mattress." —from the introduction
ISBN 978-1-57344-193-3 $15.95

Best Erotica Series

"Gets racier every year."—*San Francisco Bay Guardian*

Buy 4 books,
Get 1 *FREE**

Best Women's Erotica 2014
Edited by Violet Blue
ISBN 978-1-62778-003-2 $15.95

Best Women's Erotica 2013
Edited by Violet Blue
ISBN 978-1-57344-898-7 $15.95

Best Women's Erotica 2012
Edited by Violet Blue
ISBN 978-1-57344-755-3 $15.95

Best Bondage Erotica 2014
Edited by Rachel Kramer Bussel
ISBN 978-1-62778-012-4 $15.95

Best Bondage Erotica 2013
Edited by Rachel Kramer Bussel
ISBN 978-1-57344-897-0 $15.95

Best Bondage Erotica 2012
Edited by Rachel Kramer Bussel
ISBN 978-1-57344-754-6 $15.95

Best Lesbian Erotica 2014
Edited by Kathleen Warnock
ISBN 978-1-62778-002-5 $15.95

Best Lesbian Erotica 2013
Edited by Kathleen Warnock
Selected and introduced by
Jewelle Gomez
ISBN 978-1-57344-896-3 $15.95

Best Lesbian Erotica 2012
Edited by Kathleen Warnock
Selected and introduced by
Sinclair Sexsmith
ISBN 978-1-57344-752-2 $15.95

Best Gay Erotica 2014
Edited by Larry Duplechan
Selected and introduced by Joe Manetti
ISBN 978-1-62778-001-8 $15.95

Best Gay Erotica 2013
Edited by Richard Labonté
Selected and introduced by Paul Russell
ISBN 978-1-57344-895-6 $15.95

Best Gay Erotica 2012
Edited by Richard Labonté
Selected and introduced by
Larry Duplechan
ISBN 978-1-57344-753-9 $15.95

Best Fetish Erotica
Edited by Cara Bruce
ISBN 978-1-57344-355-5 $15.95

Best Bisexual Women's Erotica
Edited by Cara Bruce
ISBN 978-1-57344-320-3 $15.95

Best Lesbian Bondage Erotica
Edited by Tristan Taormino
ISBN 978-1-57344-287-9 $16.95

* Free book of equal or lesser value. Shipping and applicable sales tax extra.
Cleis Press • (800) 780-2279 • orders@cleispress.com
www.cleispress.com

Fuel Your Fantasies

Carnal Machines
Steampunk Erotica
Edited by D. L. King

In this decadent fusing of technology and romance, outstanding contemporary erotica writers use the enthralling possibilities of the 19th-century steam age to tease and titillate.
ISBN 978-1-57344-654-9 $14.95

The Sweetest Kiss
Ravishing Vampire Erotica
Edited by D. L. King

These sanguine tales give new meaning to the term "dead sexy" and feature beautiful bloodsuckers whose desires go far beyond blood.
ISBN 978-1-57344-371-5 $15.95

The Handsome Prince
Gay Erotic Romance
Edited by Neil Plakcy

A bawdy collection of bedtime stories brimming with classic fairy tale characters, reimagined and recast for any man who has dreamt of the day his prince will come. These sexy stories fuel fantasies and remind us all of the power of true romance.
ISBN 978-1-57344-659-4 $14.95

Daughters of Darkness
Lesbian Vampire Tales
Edited by Pam Keesey

"A tribute to the sexually aggressive woman and her archetypal roles, from nurturing goddess to dangerous predator."
—*The Advocate*
ISBN 978-1-57344-233-6 $14.95

Dark Angels
Lesbian Vampire Erotica
Edited by Pam Keesey

Dark Angels collects tales of lesbian vampires, the quintessential bad girls, archetypes of passion and terror. These tales of desire are so sharply erotic you'll swear you've been bitten!
ISBN 978-1-57344-252-7 $13.95

Out of This World Romance

Ordering is easy! Call us toll free or fax us to place your MC/VISA order. You can also mail the order form below with payment to: Cleis Press, 2246 Sixth St., Berkeley, CA 94710.

ORDER FORM

QTY	TITLE	PRICE

SUBTOTAL _____

SHIPPING _____

SALES TAX _____

TOTAL _____

Add $3.95 postage/handling for the first book ordered and $1.00 for each additional book. Outside North America, please contact us for shipping rates. California residents add 9% sales tax. Payment in U.S. dollars only.

* Free book of equal or lesser value. Shipping and applicable sales tax extra.

Cleis Press • Phone: (800) 780-2279 • Fax: (510) 845-8001
orders@cleispress.com • www.cleispress.com
You'll find more great books on our website

Follow us on Twitter @cleispress • Friend/fan us on Facebook